Heather from Nannie
Christmas 1959.

THE BOBBSEY TWINS
ON BLUEBERRY ISLAND

"Oh, Bert!" cried Freddie. *"It's here! It's come!"*

The Bobbsey Twins on Blueberry Island

By

LAURA LEE HOPE

Published by
WORLD DISTRIBUTORS (MANCHESTER) LIMITED
LONDON - MANCHESTER
ENGLAND

THE BOBBSEY TWINS BOOKS

By Laura Lee Hope

First impression 1955
Reprinted   1956
Reprinted   1957
Reprinted   1958

CONTENTS

CHAPTER I

THE GYPSIES

"OH dear! I wish we weren't going home!"

"So do I! Can't we stay out a little while longer?"

"Why, Flossie and Freddie Bobbsey!" cried Nan, the elder sister of the two small twins who had spoken. "A few minutes ago you were in a hurry to get home."

"Yes, they said they were so hungry they couldn't wait to see what Dinah was going to have for supper," said Bert Bobbsey. "How about that, Freddie?"

"Well, I'm hungry yet," said the little boy, who was sitting beside his sister Flossie in a boat that was being rowed over the blue waters of Lake Metoka. "I am hungry, and I want some of Dinah's pie, but I'd like to stay out longer."

"So would I," added Flossie. "It's so nice on the lake, and maybe tomorrow it will rain."

"Well, what if it does?" asked Nan. "You didn't expect to come out on the lake again tomorrow, did you?"

"Maybe," answered Flossie, as she smoothed out the dress of a doll she was holding in her lap.

"I'd like to come out on the lake and have a

7

picnic every day," said Freddie, leaning over the edge of the boat to see if a small ship, to which he had fastened a string, was being pulled along safely.

"Don't do that!" cried Nan quickly. "Do you want to fall in?"

"No," answered Freddie slowly, as though he had been thinking that perhaps a bath in the lake might not be so bad after all. "No, I don't want to fall in now, 'cause whenever I go in swimming I get terrible hungry, and I don't want to be any hungrier than I am now."

"Oh, so that's the only reason, is it?" asked Bert with a laugh. "Well, just keep inside the boat until we get on shore, and then you can fall out if you want to."

"How am I going to fall out when the boat's on shore?" asked Freddie. "Boats can't go on land anyhow, Bert Bobbsey!"

"That will be something for you to think about, and then maybe you won't lean over and scare Nan," said Bert, smiling.

"Do you want me to land you at your father's lumber dock, or shall I row on down near the house, Bert?" asked the man who was pulling at the oars of the boat. "It won't make any difference to me."

"Then, Jack, row us down near the house, if you don't mind," begged Nan. "I want to get these two fat twins ashore as soon as I can; Freddie especially, if he's going to almost fall overboard when I'm not looking."

"I'm not going to fall overboard!" cried the little fellow. "Can't I row, Jack?"

"Not now, Freddie. I'm in a hurry," answered Jack, as the twins called Mr. Henderson, the man whom their father had sent from the lumber-yard to manage the boat.

"Why?" asked Freddie.

"Well—er—ahem—I haven't time to let you row, Freddie. Maybe I will some other day." And Jack looked at Bert and smiled.

"Well, here you are, safe on shore!" said Jack, a short while later, when the boat had reached the landing.

"Yes, and there goes Freddie—falling overboard!" cried Bert with a laugh, as his little fat brother stumbled over a coil of rope on the dock and tumbled into the water. "It's a good thing you didn't do that in the boat, little fat fireman."

"I didn't hurt myself, anyhow," said Freddie, as he got up. "Come on, Flossie, let's run home. I'm terrible hungry."

"So'm I," added his sister, who was as fat as he, and just the same size. The two smaller Bobbsey twins started on ahead. Bert, after tying up the boat, followed on more slowly with his sister Nan.

"It was a nice ride we had," Nan said, "wasn't it, Bert?"

"Yes, it's great out on the lake. I wonder if we'll ever go camping this summer as we talked of when we were in New York?"

"Maybe. Let's tease Mother to let us!"

"All right. You ask her and I'll ask Dad. There's one island in the lake where——"

But Bert did not have a chance to finish what he was going to say, for just then Flossie and Freddie, who had hurried on ahead, came running back, surprise showing on their faces.

"Oh, Bert!" cried Freddie. "It's here! Its come!"

"Can we go to see it?" added Flossie. "Oh, I want to!"

"What's here? What do you want to see? What is it?" asked Bert and Nan together, taking turns at the questions.

"The circus is here!" answered Freddie.

"Circus?" asked Bert in surprise.

"Yes! We saw the wagons!" went on Flossie. "They're all red and yellow, and they've got mirrors all over the sides, and they have rumbly wheels like thunder, and horses with bells and——"

"You'd better save a little of your breath to eat some of the good things you think Dinah is going to cook for you," said Nan with a laugh, as she put her arms around her small sister. "Now, what is it all about?"

"It's a circus!" cried Freddie.

"We saw the wagons going along the street where our house is," added Flossie. "All red and yellow and—— Oh, look!" she suddenly cried. "There they are now!"

She pointed excitedly down the side street, on which the Bobbsey twins stood, towards the main street of Lakeport, where the Bobbsey family lived.

Nan and Bert, as well as Flossie and Freddie, saw three or four big wagons, gaily painted red and yellow, and with glittering pieces of mirror on their sides. The prancing horses drawing the wagons had bells around their necks and a merry, tinkling jingle sounded, making music wherever the horses went.

"There," said Flossie. "Isn't that a circus?"

"They certainly are circus wagons," Nan admitted.

"And pretty soon the elephants will come past," Freddie declared. "I like elephants."

"You won't see any elephants today," said Bert. "That isn't a circus parade."

"Then what is it?" Flossie demanded.

"Gypsies," Bert said. "I heard they were in the neighbourhood somewhere. Gypsies, you know," he told the small twins, "are great outdoor people. They wear rings in their ears and travel all over the country. Generally, they live in trailers, but I guess they must have bought these circus wagons because they love colourful things."

"They tell fortunes, too," Nan said. "I wanted to have my fortune told by a gypsy once, but Mother wouldn't let me," she added.

"It's silly!" declared Bert. "Just as if a gypsy could tell you what's going to happen!"

"Well, Lillie Kent had hers told," went on Nan, "and the gypsy looked at her hand and said she was going to have trouble, and she did."

"What?" asked Flossie eagerly.

"She lost a threepenny-piece a week after that—a threepenny-piece she was going to buy a lead pencil with."

"Pooh!" laughed Bert. "She'd have lost the threepenny-piece anyhow. But say, there are lots of gypsies in this band! I've counted five wagons so far."

"Maybe they're going to have a circus," insisted Freddie, who did not like to give up the idea of seeing a show.

"Course they're going to have a circus," said Flossie. "Look at all the horses." For behind the last two wagons trotted a number of horses being led by men seated on the tailboards of the bright-coloured wagons. The men had straps which were fastened to the bridles of the animals.

"No, gypsies don't give shows. They buy and sell horses," said Bert. "I've seen 'em here in Lakeport before, but not so many as this. I guess they're going to make a camp somewhere on Lake Metoka."

"Maybe we'll see 'em when we go camping," said Freddie.

"It isn't yet sure that we're going," returned Nan. "But come on. There are no more gypsy wagons to see, and we must get home."

Flossie and Freddie, somewhat disappointed that, after all, it was not a circus procession they had seen, started off again. They wished they could have seen more of the gypsies, but the gay wagons rumbled on out of sight.

"Well, we had a good time, anyhow," said

Freddie to Flossie. "And we *almost* saw a circus, didn't we?"

"Yes," answered his sister. "I'm going to be a gypsy when I grow up."

"Why?" asked Freddie.

"'Cause they've got so many mirrors on their wagons."

"I'm going to be a gypsy, too," decided Freddie, after thinking it over a bit. "'Cause they've got so many horses. I'm going to ride horseback, and you can ride in one of the wagons, Flossie."

"No. I'm going to ride horseback, too," declared the little girl. "I'm going to have a spangly thing in my hair and wear a dress all glittery and stand on the horse's back and ride——"

"Gypsies don't do that," protested Bert. "It's the people in circuses that ride standing up."

"Gypsies do too," declared Freddie, not knowing a thing about it but feeling he must back up anything Flossie said.

"No, they don't, either."

"Well, maybe they have gypsies in a circus."

"I don't believe they do," put in Nan. "Gypsies wouldn't like to be in a tent and work every afternoon and every evening. They want to keep moving on and spend lots of time out of doors."

"Well, maybe we'll be gypsies and maybe we'll be in a circus," said Freddie. "We'll see, won't we, Flossie?"

"Yes."

By this time the Bobbsey twins had turned the corner of the street leading from the lake, and were in sight of their home. What they saw caused Bert, Nan, Flossie, and Freddie to set out at a run. In front of their house was a crowd of people. There were men, women, and children, and among them the twins could see their mother, Dinah, the cook, and Sam Johnson, her husband, who drove Mr. Bobbsey's lumber-trucks.

"What's the matter?" asked Nan.

"Something has happened!" cried Bert.

"The house is on fire!" shouted Freddie. "I must get my fire engine that squirts real water!" and he raced on ahead.

"Wait a minute!" called Bert.

The Bobbsey twins saw their mother coming quickly towards them. She held out her arms and cried: "Oh, I'm so glad you're safe!"

"Why, what's the matter?" asked Flossie.

"Helen Porter can't be found," Mrs. Bobbsey answered. "Her mother has looked everywhere for her, but can't find her."

"She's been carried off by the gypsies!" exclaimed John Marsh, an excited boy about Bert's age. "The gypsies took her! I saw 'em!"

"You did?" asked Bert.

"Sure I did! A man! Dark, with a red sash on, and gold rings in his ears! He picked Helen up in his arms and went off with her! She's in one of the gypsy wagons now!"

When John said this, Flossie and Freddie huddled closer to their mother.

CHAPTER II

A SURPRISE

"WHAT'S all this? What's the matter?" asked a voice on the outside fringe of the crowd that had gathered in front of the Bobbsey home. Looking up, Bert saw his father coming down the street from the direction of his lumber-yard. "Has anything happened?" asked Mr. Bobbsey, after a glance had shown him that his own little family was safe.

"Lots of things have happened, Mr. Bobbsey," answered Dinah. "Oh, the poor honey lamb! Just to think of it!"

"But who is it? What has happened?" asked Mr. Bobbsey, looking about for someone to answer him. Flossie and Freddie decided they would do this.

"It's gypsies," said the little "fat fireman", as his father sometimes called Freddie.

"And they carried off Helen Porter," added the little "fat fairy", which was Flossie's pet name. "An' I saw the wagons, all mirrors, an' Freddie an' I are goin' to be gypsies when we grow up." Flossie was so excited that she dropped a lot of "g" letters from the ends of words where they belonged.

"You don't mean to say that the gypsies have

carried off Helen Porter—the little girl who lives next door?" asked Mr. Bobbsey in great surprise.

"Yes! They did! I saw 'em!" exclaimed John Marsh. "She had curly hair, and when the gypsy man took her in his arms she cried, Helen did!"

"Oh!" exclaimed Flossie, Freddie, and other children in the crowd.

"There must be some mistake," said Mr. Bobbsey. "Those gypsies would never take away a child, even in fun, in broad daylight. It must be a mistake. Let me hear more about it."

And while the father of the Bobbsey twins is trying to find out just what had happened, I will take a few minutes to let my readers know something of the twins themselves, for this book is about them.

To begin with there were four Bobbsey twins, as you have guessed before this. Nan and Bert were twelve years old, tall and dark, with eyes and hair to match. Flossie and Freddie were six, short and fat, and they had light hair and blue eyes.

With their mother and their father, who owned a large lumber-yard, the twins lived in the eastern city of Lakeport near the head of Lake Metoka. There were others in the family besides the twins and their parents. There was dear old Dinah, the cook, who made such good pies, and there was Sam, her husband. And I must not forget Snoop, the black cat, nor Snap, the big dog, who once did tricks in a circus.

"But now let me hear what it is all about," said Mr. Bobbsey, who had come home from the office of his lumber-yard to find an excited crowd in front of his house. "Were there really any gypsies?" he asked Mrs. Bobbsey. "And did they take away Helen Porter?"

"I don't know about that last part," said Mrs. Bobbsey, "but a caravan of gypsies did pass by the house a little while ago. I heard Dinah say something about the gaily painted wagons, and I looked out in time to see them rumbling along the street. Then, a little later, I heard Mrs. Porter calling for Helen, and, on seeing the crowd, I ran out. I was worried about our children until I saw them coming from the lake, where they had gone for a row in the boat."

"I can't believe that gypsies took Helen," said Mr. Bobbsey.

"Oh, but she's *gone!*" several neighbours told him. "We can't find her *anywhere*, and her mother is crying terribly!"

"Well, it may be that Helen is lost, or has even strayed away after the gypsies, thinking their wagons were part of a circus, as Nan says Flossie thought," said Mr. Bobbsey. "But gypsies wouldn't dare take a little girl away in broad daylight."

As he said this he looked at his own little children and at others in the crowd, for he did not want them to be frightened.

"Years ago, maybe, gypsies did take little folks," he said, "but they don't do it any more, I'm sure."

"But where is Helen?" asked John Marsh. "A gypsy man has her, I know, 'cause I saw him take her."

"Are you sure?" asked Mr. Bobbsey, for John was an excitable boy, sometimes given to imagining things that never happened.

"Course I'm sure," he said. "Cross my heart!" and he did so, while the other children looked on wonderingly.

"Suppose you go over to Mrs. Porter's house," said Mrs. Bobbsey to the children's father. "She's so worried, and her husband isn't home yet. Maybe you can help her. I was just going in when you came along."

"All right, I'll go," said Mr. Bobbsey.

"Can't we come?" asked Freddie, and as he had hold of his little sister's hand, it was Flossie, of course, whom he included in his question.

"No, you must go with your mother," said his father, and when the "little fat fireman" seemed disappointed Mr. Bobbsey went on: "I guess supper is almost ready, isn't it, Dinah?"

"Indeed it is, and there's pudding with grated maple sugar sprinkled over the top."

"Oh, I want some of *that!*" cried Flossie. "Come on, Freddie! We can look for the gypsies after supper."

"And we'll get Helen out of the shiny wagons," added Freddie, as he hurried towards the Bobbsey home with Flossie, Dinah waddling along after them.

"I'll go with you," offered Bert to his father. "Maybe you might want me to go on an errand."

"Yes, take Bert with you," said Mrs. Bobbsey. "I'll look after Nan, Flossie, and Freddie. And be sure to tell Mrs. Porter that if I can do anything for her I will."

"I'll tell her," and then Mr. Bobbsey, with Bert, walked to the Porter house next door.

The crowd in the street grew larger, and there was much talk about the gypsies. Some said that several little boys and girls had been carried off, but, of course, this was not so.

As Flossie and Freddie hurried on towards the house in front of Dinah, they continued to chatter about the gypsies.

"If gypsies take little girls we don't want to be them—the gypsies, I mean—Freddie."

"Humph-umph; that's so. Well, I guess we'll be in a circus anyhow. That'll be more fun. You can ride a horse in the ring, and sometimes I can ride with you and sometimes I can be a clown. When I'm a clown I can squirt water from my fire engine over the other clowns. That'll make the folks shout and laugh."

When Nan and Mrs. Bobbsey reached the house each of the little twins was munching on a piece of maple sugar, given them by Dinah to keep them from nibbling at the pudding before the time to serve it came.

"My, Mummy! Aren't you glad the gypsies came and got Helen Porter? It gives us something to think about," remarked Freddie coolly.

"Freddie Bobbsey!" gasped his mother. "No, I am not glad the gypsies got Helen—if they did. And you and Flossie find enough to think about, as it is."

"There go Daddy and Bert into Mrs. Porter's house now," said Nan.

"Now tell me just what happened, and I'll do all I can to help you," said Mr. Bobbsey to Mrs. Porter, when he got to her house and found her half-crying in the living-room where there were a number of other women.

"Oh, Helen is gone, I'm sure she is!" cried the mother. "The gypsies have taken her! I'll never see her again!"

"Oh, yes, you will," said Mr. Bobbsey in mild tones. "I'm sure it's all a mistake. The gypsies haven't taken her at all. Why do you think so?"

"Johnnie Marsh saw them carry her away!"

"Then let's have Johnnie in here where we can talk to him. Bert, suppose you do one of those errands you spoke of," said his father with a smile, "and bring Johnnie in out of the crowd where I can talk to him quietly."

John, or Johnnie, as he was often called, was quite ready to come when Bert found him outside the Porter house, telling over and over again to a crowd of boys what he had seen, or what he thought he had seen.

"Now tell us just what happened," said Mr. Bobbsey, when the small boy was seated in a chair in the Porter living-room.

"Well, I was coming from the store for my mother," said Johnnie, "and I saw the gypsy wagons. I thought it was a circus."

"That's what Flossie and Freddie thought," said Bert to his father.

"But it wasn't," went on Johnnie. "Then I saw Helen playing in Grace Lavine's garden down the street when I came past. And a little while after that, when I had to go to the store for my mother again, 'cause I forgot the yeast cakes, I saw a gypsy man running along the street and he had Helen in his arms and she was crying."

"What made you think it was Helen?" asked Mr. Bobbsey.

" 'Cause I saw her light hair. Helen's got fluffy hair like your Flossie's."

"Yes, I know she has," said Mr. Bobbsey. "What did you do when you thought you saw the gypsy man carrying Helen away?" and they all waited anxiously for Johnnie's answer.

"I ran home," said Johnnie. "I didn't want to be carried off in one of those funny-looking wagons."

"Quite right," said Mr. Bobbsey. "Then you really didn't see the gypsy man pick Helen up in his arms?"

"No," slowly answered the little boy, "he only just ran past me. But he must have picked her up in Grace's garden, for that's where Helen was playing."

"Then we'd better go down to where Grace Lavine lives and see what she can tell us," said Mr. Bobbsey.

"You don't need to," put in Bert. "I see Grace out in front now with some other girls. Shall I call her in?"

"Oh, please do!" exclaimed Mrs. Porter. "My poor Helen! Oh, what has happened to her?"

"We'll get your little girl back, even if the gypsies have her," said Mr. Bobbsey. "But I don't believe they have taken her away. Call in Grace, Bert."

Grace was not as excited as Johnnie, and told what she knew.

"Helen and Mary Benson and I were playing in my garden," said Grace. "We had our dolls and were having a tea-party. Mary and I went into the house to get some biscuits, to play they were strawberry shortcake, and we left Helen out under the trees with her doll. When we came back she wasn't there nor her doll either, and down the street we saw the gypsy wagons."

"Did you see any gypsy man come into the garden and get Helen?" asked Mr. Bobbsey.

"No," said Grace, shaking her head, "I didn't. But the gypsies must have taken her, 'cause she was gone."

"Oh, please, someone go after the gypsies, and make a search among them, at any rate!" cried Mrs. Porter.

"We'll get right after them," said Mr. Bobbsey. "I don't really believe the gypsies took Helen, but they may have seen her. They can't have gone on very far. I'll call some policemen and we'll get after them."

"I'll come with you," said Bert. "Maybe we'd better get our car."

"It would be a good idea," said his father. "Let me see now. I think——"

But before Mr. Bobbsey could say what he thought there was the sound of shouts in the street, and when those in the Porter home rushed to the windows and doors they were surprised to see, coming up the front path, the missing little girl herself!

There was Helen Porter, not carried off by the gypsies at all, but safe at home; though something had happened, that was sure, for she was crying.

"Here she is! Here she is!" cried several in the crowd, and Mrs. Porter rushed out to hug her little girl close in her arms.

CHAPTER III

WORRIED TWINS

"OH, Helen! how glad I am to have you back!" cried Mrs. Porter. "How did you get away from the gypsies? Or did they really have you?"

The little girl stopped crying, and all about her the men, women, and children waited anxiously to hear what she would say.

"Did the gypsies take you away?" asked Mr. Bobbsey.

"No, the gypsies didn't get me," said Helen, her voice now and then broken by sobs. "But they took Mollie!"

"Took Mollie!" cried Mr. Bobbsey. "Do you mean to say they really did take a little girl away?"

"They—they took Mollie!" half-sobbed Helen, "and I—I tried to get her back, but I couldn't run fast enough and—and——"

"Well, if they really have Mollie," went on Mr. Bobbsey, "we must get right after them and——"

"Mollie is the name of Helen's big doll—almost as large as she is," explained Mrs. Porter, who was now smiling through her tears. "Mollie isn't a little girl, though probably there are several in Lakeport named that. But the Mollie whom Helen means is a doll."

"Oh, I see," said Mr. Bobbsey. "But did the gypsies really take your doll, Helen?"

"Yes, they did," answered the little girl. "A bad gypsy man took her away. I was playing with Mollie in Grace Lavine's garden, and Grace and Mary went into the house to get some biscuits. I stayed out in the yard with my doll, 'cause I wanted her to get tanned nice and brown. I laid her down in a sunny place, and I went over under a tree to set the tea-table, and when I looked around I saw the gypsy man."

"Where was he?" asked Mr. Bobbsey.

"He was just getting out of one of the red wagons. And there was a little gypsy girl in the wagon. She was pointing to my doll, and then the man jumped down off the wagon steps, ran into the garden, picked up my doll, and then he jumped into the wagon again and rode away. And he's got my nice doll Mollie, and I want her back, and—oh dear!" and Helen began to cry again.

"Never mind," said Mr. Bobbsey quietly. "I'll try to get your doll back again. How large was it?"

"Nearly as large as Helen herself," said Mrs. Porter. "I didn't want her to play with it today, but she took it."

"Yes, but now the gypsy man with rings in his ears—he took it," explained Helen. "He carried my doll off in his arms."

"Just so," agreed Mr. Bobbsey. "Seeing the doll in the garden, with no one near, the gypsy man made up his mind to take her for his own little girl. This he did, and when he ran off with Mollie,

Johnnie saw what happened and thought Helen was being kidnapped.

"But I'm glad that wasn't so, though it's too bad Mollie has been taken away. However, we'll try to get her back for you, Helen. Maybe the gypsies took other things. If they did we'll send the police after them. Now don't cry any more and I'll see what I can do."

"And will you get Mollie back?"

"I'll do my best," promised the Bobbsey twins' father.

There being nothing more he could do just then at the Porter home, Mr. Bobbsey went back to his own family, and told Mrs. Bobbsey, Flossie, Freddie, and Nan what had happened.

"Oh, I'm so glad Helen is all right," said Mrs. Bobbsey.

"But it's too bad about her doll," sighed Nan. She had a doll of her own—a fine one—and she knew how she would feel if she had been taken.

"Helen's doll could talk," said Flossie. "I know, 'cause she let me make it talk one day. You wind up a winder thing in her back, and then you push on a button in her front and she says 'Mamma' and 'Papa' and other things."

"Yes, that's right," said Nan. "Mollie is a talking doll. I guess she has a little gramophone inside her. Maybe that's the noise Johnnie heard when the gypsy man carried the doll past him, and Johnnie thought it was Helen crying."

"I guess that was it," agreed Mr. Bobbsey. "Well, it's too bad to lose a big talking doll. I must see what I can do to help get it back. I'll call up the chief of police."

"It would be worse to lose your toy fire engine," declared Freddie.

"Why, Freddie Bobbsey!" exclaimed his little sister, "nothing could be worse than to lose your very best doll—your very own child!"

Mr. Bobbsey, being one of the most prominent businessmen in the town, had considerable business at times with the police and the fire departments, and the officers would do almost anything to help him or his friends.

So, after supper—at which Dinah had served the pudding with the grated maple sugar over the top, Flossie and Freddie each having had two helpings—Mr. Bobbsey called up the police station and asked if anything more had been heard of the gypsies.

"Well, yes, we did hear something of them," answered Chief Branford, over the telephone. "They've gone into camp, where they always do, on the western shore of the lake, and as I've had several reports of small things having been stolen around town, I'm going to send an officer out there to the gypsy camp, and have him see what he can find. You say they took your little girl's doll?"

"No, not my little girl's," answered Mr. Bobbsey, "but the talking doll belonging to a friend of hers."

"Her name is Mollie, Daddy," said Flossie, who, with the other Bobbsey twins, was listening to her father talk over the telephone. "I mean the doll's name is Mollie, not Helen's name."

"I understand," said Mr. Bobbsey with a laugh, and he told the chief the name of the doll and also the name of the little girl who owned it.

"Well, what is to be done?" asked Mrs. Bobbsey, as her husband hung up.

"I think I'll go with the policeman and see what I can find out about the gypsies," said Mr. Bobbsey. "If they are going to take things that do not belong to them, they may pay a visit to my lumber-yard, if they have not done so already. I think I'll go out to the gypsy camp."

"Oh, let me come!" begged Bert, always ready for an adventure.

"I wouldn't go—not at night, anyhow," remarked Nan.

"Nor I," added Freddie, while Flossie crept up into her mother's lap.

"Oh, I'm not going until morning," said Mr. Bobbsey. "Then I'll take you, Bert, if you'd like to go. We'll see if we can find Helen's big talking doll."

"She must feel bad at losing it," said Nan.

"She does," said Bert. "Though how anyone can get to like a doll, I can't see."

"They're as good as nasty old knives that cut you, and kite strings that are always getting tangled," said Nan with a laugh.

"Yes, I guess we like different things," agreed her brother. "Well, I'm glad it wasn't Flossie or Freddie the gypsies took away with them."

"I wouldn't go!" declared Freddie. "And if they took Flossie, I'd get my fire engine and squirt water on those men with rings in their ears till they let my sister go!"

"That's my little fat fireman!" laughed Mr. Bobbsey. "But now I think you're getting sleepy. Your row on the lake made the sandman come around earlier than usual, I guess. Off to bed with you."

Flossie and Freddie went to bed earlier than Nan and Bert, who were allowed to sit up a little later. There was much talk about the gypsies, and what they might have taken, and Nan and Bert were getting ready for bed when a pattering of bare feet was heard on the stairs and a voice called:

"Where's Snoop?"

"Why, it's Flossie and Freddie!" cried Mrs. Bobbsey, as she saw the two small twins. "Why are you out of bed?" she asked.

"Freddie thought maybe the gypsies would take our cat Snoop," explained Flossie, "so we got up to ask you to bring him in."

"And bring in Snap, our dog," added Freddie. "The gypsies might take him, 'cause he does tricks and was once in a circus."

"Oh, don't worry about that!" laughed Mr. Bobbsey. "Get back to bed before you catch cold."

"But you won't let the gypsies take them, will you?" asked Flossie anxiously.

"No, indeed!" promised her mother. "Snoop is safely curled up in his basket, and I guess Snap wouldn't let a gypsy come near him."

But Flossie and Freddie were not satisfied until they had looked and had seen the big black cat cosily asleep, and had heard Snap bark outside when Bert called to him from a window.

"The gypsies won't take your pets," their father told the small twins, and then, hand in hand, they went upstairs again to bed.

CHAPTER IV

THE GOAT

"CAN'T we come, too?"

"We're not afraid of the gypsies—not in day-time."

Flossie and Freddie thus called after their father and Bert, as they started the next morning to go to find the gypsy camp. The night had passed quietly, and Snap and Snoop were found safe when day dawned. After breakfast, Mr. Bobbsey and his older son were to go to Lake Metoka and find where the gypsies had stopped with the gay red and yellow wagons. They were going to see if they could find any trace of Helen's doll, and also things belonging to other people in town, which it was thought the gypsy visitors might have taken.

"Please let us go?" begged the little Bobbsey twins.

"Oh, my dears, no!" said Mrs. Bobbsey. "It's too far; and besides——"

"Are you afraid the gypsies will carry us off?" asked Freddie. "'Cause if you are I'll take my fire engine, and some of the funny beetles that go around and around and around that we got in New York, and I'll scare the gypsies with 'em and squirt water on 'em."

"No, I'm not afraid of you or Flossie's being carried off—especially when your father is with you," said Mrs. Bobbsey. "But there is no telling where the gypsies are camped, and it may be a long walk before they are found. So you stay with me, and I'll get Dinah to let you have a party."

"Oh, that will be fun!" cried Flossie.

"I'd rather play hunt gypsies," said her brother, but when he saw Dinah come out of the kitchen with a tiny little cake she had baked especially for him and his sister to have a play-party with, Freddie thought, after all, there was some fun in staying at home.

"But take Snap with you," he said to Bert. "He'll growl at the gypsy men, and maybe he'll scare 'em so they'll give back Helen's doll."

"Well, Snap can growl hard when he wants to," said Bert with a laugh. "But still I think it wouldn't be a good thing to take him to the gypsy camp. They nearly always have dogs in their camp— the gypsies do—and those dogs might get into a fight with Snap."

"Snap could beat 'em!" declared Freddie.

"No, don't take him!" ordered Flossie. "I don't want Snap to get bit."

"I don't either," agreed Bert, "so I'll leave him at home, I guess. Well, there's Dad calling me. I'll have to run. I'll tell you all about it when I come back."

So, while Flossie and Freddie, with the little cake Dinah had baked for them, went to have a good time playing party, Mr. Bobbsey, with a policeman and Bert, went to the gypsy camp. The policeman did not have on his uniform—in fact, he was dressed almost like Mr. Bobbsey.

"For," said this policeman, whose name was Joseph Carr, "if the gypsy men were to see me coming along in my uniform, they would know right away who I was. They would hide away that little girl's doll, or anything else they may have taken. So I'm going in plain clothes."

"Like a detective," said Bert.

"Yes, something like a detective," agreed Mr. Carr. "Now let's step along lively."

Several persons had seen the gypsy caravan of gay yellow and red wagons going through Lakeport, and had noticed them turn up along the farther shore of Lake Metoka. There was a patch of wood several miles away from the town, and in years past these same gypsies, or others like them, had camped there. It was to these woods that Bert and his father were going.

"Do you think we'll find Helen's doll?" asked the boy.

"Well, maybe, Bert," answered his father. "And maybe the gypsies have it, and won't give it up. We'll just have to wait and see."

"If I get sight of it they'll give it up soon enough," said Policeman Carr.

After about a two-hour walk, Bert, his father, and Mr. Carr came to the woods. Through the trees they looked and saw the red and yellow wagons standing in a circle. Near them were tied a number of horses, eating what little grass grew under the trees, while dogs roamed about here and there.

"I'm glad we didn't bring Snap," said Bert. "There'd have been a dog fight as sure as fate."

"Yes, I guess so," agreed his father.

By this time they had entered the gypsy camp, and some of the dark-faced men, with dangling gold rings in their ears, came walking slowly forward to ask the two visitors with the young boy what was wanted.

"We're after a big doll," said Mr. Bobbsey. "One was taken from a little girl in our town yesterday. Perhaps you gypsies took it by mistake, and, if so, we'd be glad to have it back."

"We haven't any doll," growled one big gypsy. "We have only what is our own."

"I'm not so sure about that," said Mr. Carr. "We'll have a look about the camp and see what we can find."

"You are wasting your time here," said this gypsy, who seemed to be the leader, or "king", as he is sometimes called. "We have nothing but what is our own. We have no little girl's doll."

"We'll have a look about," said Mr. Carr again.

But though the policeman and Mr. Bobbsey, to say nothing of Bert, who had very sharp eyes, looked all about the gypsy camp, there was no sign of the missing doll. If a gypsy man had taken it, he had either hidden it well or, possibly, had gone off to some other camp.

"If the doll would only talk now and tell us where she is, we could get her," said Bert with a laugh to his father, when they had walked through the camp and come out on the other side.

"That's right," agreed Mr. Bobbsey, "but I'm afraid the doll isn't smart enough for that. Do you see anything else that the gypsies may have taken?" asked the twins' father of the policeman.

"I'm not sure," answered Mr. Carr. "We had a report of two horses missing, and they may be here, but most horses look so much alike to me that I can't tell them apart. I guess I'll have to get the men who own them to come here and see if they can pick them out."

For half an hour Bert, his father, and Mr. Carr roamed through the gypsy camp, the dark-faced men and women scowling at them, and the dogs barking. If there were any boys or girls in the camp Bert did not see them, and he thought they might be hiding.

"Well, we didn't find the doll," said Mr. Carr when they were on their way back to Lakeport. "But I'm sure some of the horses the gypsies have don't belong to them. The chief of police is going to make them move away from that camp anyhow, for the man who owns the land doesn't like the gypsies there. He says they take his neighbours' chickens."

Flossie and Freddie, as well as Helen Porter, were much disappointed when Mr. Bobbsey and Bert came back without the doll. Helen was sure some gypsy had it, but as it could not be found, nothing could be done about it.

"We'll help you look some more this afternoon,"

Freddie said to Helen, into whose eyes tears came whenever she thought of her lost doll. "Maybe you left Mollie under some bush in Grace's garden."

"I looked under all the bushes," said Helen.

"Well, we'll look again," promised Freddie, and they did, but no doll was found.

The next day the gypsies were made to move on with their gaily coloured wagons, their horses and dogs, and though they went (for they had no right to camp on the land near the lake), they were very angry about it.

"They said they had camped there for many years," reported Mr. Carr, telling about the police having driven the gypsy men and women away, "and that they would make whoever it was that drove them away sorry that he had done such a thing."

"I suppose that means," said Mr. Bobbsey, "that they'll help themselves from somebody's chicken coop."

"We haven't got any chickens," said Freddie

"But we've got a dog and a cat," put in Flossie. "If those gypsies take Snap or Snoop I—I'll go after 'em, I will!"

"So'll I!" declared her little fat brother.

"What'll you do when you get to where the gypsies are?" asked Bert.

"Why, I—I'll——" began Freddie.

"Oh, I'll just pick Snoop up in my arms and tell Snap to come with me and we'll run home," answered Flossie.

"But maybe the gypsies——"

"Don't, Bert," admonished his father. "I do not believe that you little twins need worry about your cat and your dog," he continued.

Still, for several days and nights after that Flossie and Freddie were very much worried lest their pets should be taken away. But the gypsies did not come back again—at least for a time, and though the small Bobbsey twins again helped Helen hunt under many bushes for her talking doll it could not be found.

"I just *know* the gypsy man took my Mollie!" declared Helen.

It was about a week after this (and summer seemed to have come all of a sudden) that, when the mail came one morning, Mrs. Bobbsey saw a postcard that made her smile as she read it.

"What's it about, Mumsie?" asked Freddie, when he noticed his mother's happy face. "Are we going back to New York?"

"No, but this postcard has something to do with something that happened in New York," was Mrs. Bobbsey's answer. "It is from the express company to your father, and it says there is, at the express office, a——"

Just then Mrs. Bobbsey dropped the postcard, and as Nan picked it up to hand to her mother the little girl saw one word.

"Oh!" cried Nan, "it's about a goat!"

"A—a goat?" gasped Flossie.

"A goat!" shouted Freddie. "A live goat!"

"Why—er—yes—I guess so," and Nan looked at the postcard again.

"Oh, I know!" cried Freddie. "It's that goat I almost bought in New York—Mike's goat! Oh, did Daddy get a goat for us as he promised?" Freddie asked his mother.

CHAPTER V

A BUMPY RIDE

THE Bobbsey Twins—all four of them—stood in a circle about their mother, looking eagerly at her and at the postcard which Nan had handed to her. Freddie and Flossie were smiling expectantly, while Nan and Bert looked as though they were not quite sure whether or not it was a joke.

"Is it really a goat, Mother?" asked Bert.

"Well, that's what this postcard says," answered Mrs. Bobbsey. "A goat and cart have arrived at the express office, and your father is asked to come to get them and take them away."

"Course he's got to take 'em away," said Freddie. "The goat'll be hungry there, for he can't get anything to eat."

"And he might butt somebody with his horns," added Flossie.

"Daddy wouldn't buy a butting goat," Freddie declared. "Anyhow, let's go and get him. I want to have a ride."

"If there really is a goat outfit at the express office for us," said Bert, "we'd better get it, I think. I'll take the postcard down to the lumber-yard office and ask Dad——"

"I'm going with you!" cried Freddie.

"I'm coming, too!" added Flossie.

"Suppose you all go," suggested Mrs. Bobbsey. "Your father will tell you what to do, for I'm sure I don't know what to say. I never had a goat. Four twins, a dog and a cat are about all I can manage," she said laughingly, as Dinah came into the room to ask what to order from the grocery stores.

"A goat!" exclaimed the coloured cook. "There sure will be trouble if my honey lambs take to playin' with goats!"

"I know how to drive a goat!" declared Freddie. "Mike, the red-haired boy in New York, showed me. Flossie and I had a ride in his wagon for two cents. It was fun, wasn't it, Flossie?"

"Yes. I liked it. We had lots of fun in New York. We had beetles that went around and around and around."

"Maybe the goat will go around and around and around," said Nan, half laughing.

"Well, hurry down to your father's office with the postcard," advised Mrs. Bobbsey. "He'll know what to do."

And when the four excited Bobbsey twins—for even Bert was excited over the chance of owning a goat—reached their father's office, he told them all about it.

"You remember," he said, "that when Freddie and Flossie 'almost' bought the goat in New York I promised that if I could find a good one for sale, with a harness and cart, I'd buy it for you this summer. Well, I heard of one the other day, and

I got it, and had it sent on here by express. Now we'll go down and see what it looks like."

"It's going to be my goat—Flossie's and mine, isn't it?" asked Freddie, as they started for the express office down near the railway station.

"No more yours than it will be Nan's and Bert's, my little fat fireman," said Mr. Bobbsey with a laugh. "You must all be kind to the goat and take turns riding in the cart."

"Can't we all ride at once?" asked Nan.

"Well, I don't know how large the cart is," answered Mr. Bobbsey. "Maybe you can all get in at once, that is, if the goat is strong enough to pull you."

"I hope he's a big goat," said Freddie. "Then me and Bert will drive him and give Flossie and you a ride, Nan."

"Don't let him run away with me, that's all I ask!" begged Nan, laughing.

They found the goat in a crate on the express platform. Near him was a good-sized cart.

"Oh, we can all get in it!" cried Freddie, as he ran from the cart over to where the goat was bleating in his crate. The animal was a large white one, and he seemed gentle when Flossie and Freddie put their hands in through the slats of the crate and patted him.

"I think he'd like to get out where he can walk around and have something to eat and drink," said Mr. Bobbsey. "We must take him out of his crate."

This was soon done with the help of the express agent, and, when the last piece of wood was taken off, the goat stepped out of his crate in which he had travelled from a distant city, and gave a loud "Baaa-a-a-a-a!"

Then he stamped his forefeet on the platform, and shook his head, on which were two horns.

"Oh, look out! He'll run away!" cried Freddie, who was afraid of losing his goat before there was a chance for a ride.

But the goat seemed tame, kind and gentle, and after walking about a little, stood still beside the crate and let the children pat him.

There was a piece of paper pasted on the crate in which the goat had travelled. One end of the paper was flapping loose, and, seeing it, the white animal nibbled at it, and finally ate it, chewing it up as though he liked it.

"Oh, look!" cried Nan. "The goat's eating the label off his crate so we can't send him back. He likes us, I guess."

"We like *him*, anyhow," said Freddie, laughing and patting the billy. "Come on, Bert. Hitch him up and give us a ride."

"Shall I?" asked Bert of his father.

"Why, yes, I guess so. Might as well start now as any time. The man I bought him from said he was kind and gentle and liked children. I'll show you how to harness him up, Bert."

A complete harness had come with the goat and cart. When the white animal had been given a drink of water and fed some grass which Flossie and Freddie pulled for him, Bert, helped by his father and the express agent, put the harness on.

"What are we going to call him?" asked Nan. "We'll have to have a name for our goat. We don't want to call him 'it', or 'Billy'."

"Name him Whisker," said Bert. "See, he has whiskers just like an old man."

"Oh, that's a nice, funny name!" laughed Flossie, and Freddie thought so too. So the goat was named Whisker, and he seemed to like that as well as any. What he had been called before they got him, the children did not know.

Whisker did not seem to mind being hitched to the little cart, and when Mr. Bobbsey had made sure that all the straps were well fastened, Bert took the front seat, with Nan beside him, while Flossie and Freddie sat in the back. They set off, Mr. Bobbsey walking beside the goat to make sure he did not run away.

But Whisker seemed to be a very good goat indeed, and went along nicely, and so slowly and carefully that Freddie, several times, begged to be allowed to drive.

"I will let you after a while," promised Bert. "Let me get used to him first."

When the Bobbsey twins came riding down their street in the goat-cart you can imagine how surprised all the other children were. They gathered in front of the house and rushed into the garden when Bert turned Whisker up the driveway.

"Oh, give us a ride! Give us a ride!" cried the playmates of the Bobbsey twins.

"Yes, I'll give you all rides," promised Bert.

Then began a jolly time for the Bobbsey twins

and their friends. Whisker did not seem to mind how many children he hauled around the smooth level path at the side of the house, and sometimes the cart was as full as it could be. Nor did the goat try to butt anyone with his horns, letting the boys and girls pet him as much as they pleased.

"He's almost as nice as my doll the gypsies took," said Helen Porter, after she had had a ride. "I like Whisker."

"Did you find your doll?" asked Flossie.

"No. I can't find Mollie anywhere. I just know she's been turned into a gypsy. Oh dear!"

"Flossie and I'll help you find her," promised Freddie once again. "Some day I'm going to drive the goat all alone, and I'll give you and Flossie a long ride, Helen. Then we'll go find your doll."

"That'll be nice," said Helen.

One day, soon after Bert had hitched Whisker to the cart, and was going to give his two sisters and brother a ride, a telephone message came from Mr. Bobbsey, asking Bert to come to the lumber office to get something Mr. Bobbsey had to send home to Mrs. Bobbsey.

"I'll give you a ride when I come back," promised Bert, hurrying down the street.

"We'll leave Whisker hitched up," said Nan. "I'll go in and finish sewing up that hole in my sock I was mending."

"And I'll stay out here in the goat-cart," said Freddie, while Flossie nodded her head to say she would do the same thing.

A little later, and before Bert had come back

from his father's office, Helen Porter came walking past the Bobbsey house. Looking in the garden, she saw Flossie and Freddie seated in the goat-cart.

"Come on in," invited Flossie. "We're having a make-believe ride, and you can ride too. Can't she, Freddie?"

"Yes. An' I'm going to drive—make-believe. Come on, Helen. When Bert comes I'll ask him to take us to help find the gypsies and get back your doll."

Helen hurried in and took her place in the cart, and the three children had lots of fun pretending they were going on a long trip. They did not really go, for the goat was tied to a post.

"I wish Bert would hurry back," said Flossie, after a bit. "I'm tired of staying in one place so long."

"So'm I," said Freddie. Then he got out of the cart and began loosening the strap by which the goat was fastened to the post.

"What're you doing?" Flossie asked.

"I—I just want to see what Whisker'll do," answered the little boy. "Maybe he's tired of standing still."

Indeed, the goat seemed to be, for no sooner had Freddie got into the cart again than off Whisker started, walking slowly towards the back of the garden, where there was a gate to a rear street which led to the woods.

"Whoa!" cried Freddie, but he did not say it very loudly. "Whoa, Whisker! Where you going?"

"Oh, he's running away!" cried Helen. "Let me out! He's running away!"

"No, he's only walking," said Freddie. "It's all right. As long as he walks, you won't get hurt. I guess I'd better drive him, though."

"Can't you stop him?" asked Flossie. "Bert won't like it to have us take him away."

"We aren't taking him away; he's taking *us* away," said Freddie. "I can't make him stop. Look!" Again he called: "Whoa!" but the goat did not obey.

On and on went Whisker, slowly at first, then walking a little faster and pulling after him the little cart with the children in it.

"Oh, he's going to the woods!" cried Flossie, as she saw the goat heading for the patch of trees at the end of the back street. "Stop him, Freddie!"

"Maybe he wants to go there," said Freddie. "He won't stop for me."

"But it—it's such a bumpy road," said Helen, the words being fairly jarred out of her. "It's all —all bu-bu-bumps and hu-hu-humps."

"That's 'cause we're in the woods," said Freddie for by this time the goat had drawn the cart into the shade of the woods, not far from the Bobbsey home. It was indeed a bumpy place, Whisker pulling the children over tree roots and bits of broken wood. But the cart was stout, and the goat was strong. Then, suddenly, Freddie had an idea.

"Oh, Helen!" he cried, "I guess Whisker is taking us to find your lost doll!"

CHAPTER VI

JOLLY NEWS

WHISKER, the big white goat, seemed to know exactly what he was doing. He stepped briskly along, pulling after him the cart in which the children rode. They were bumped about quite a bit, for the path through the woods was anything but smooth.

In some places there was no path at all, but this did not seem to worry Whisker. He went along anyhow, now and then stopping to nibble at some green leaves, and again turning to one side to crop some grass.

"Do you really think he's taking us to my doll?" asked Helen eagerly.

"I—I hope so," answered Flossie, somewhat doubtfully.

"Maybe he is," said Freddie. "Anyhow, the gypsies that took your doll Mollie came to the woods, and we're in the woods, and maybe the doll is here and maybe we'll find her."

That was as much as Freddie could think of at one time, especially as he had to hold the reins that were fastened to the bit in Whisker's mouth. For the goat was driven just as a horse or pony is driven, and Freddie was doing the driving this time.

At least the little boy thought he was, and that was very near the same thing. But Whisker went along by himself pretty much as he pleased, really not needing much driving by the leather reins. And he never needed to be whipped—in fact, there was not a whip in the cart, for the Bobbsey children never thought of using it. They were kind to their goat.

"Oh, I'm falling out!" suddenly cried Helen, as the goat-cart went over a very rough, bumpy place.

"Hold on tight like me," said Flossie. "Anyhow," she went on, as she looked out of the cart, "if you do fall you won't get hurt much, 'cause there's a lot of soft moss and leaves on the ground."

"But I'll get my dress dirty," said Helen.

"Then we'll go down to the lake and wash it off," said Freddie, for the woods in which they now were led down to the shore of the lake.

"Well, I don't want to fall, anyhow," said Helen. " 'Most always when I fall I bump my nose, an' it hurts."

"It's smoother now, and I guess the cart won't tip over," observed Freddie, a little later.

They had come now to a wider path in the woods, where it was not so bumpy, and the cart rolled easily over the moss and leaves as Whisker pulled it along.

"It's nice in here," said Flossie, looking about her.

"Yes, I'm glad Whisker took us for a ride," said Freddie.

"He wouldn't have if you hadn't unhitched his strap," remarked Flossie. "What'll Bert say?"

"Well, Whisker was tired of standing still," went on her brother. "And, anyhow, Helen wanted to come for a ride to find her doll; didn't you?" he asked their little playmate.

"Yes, I did," she answered. "I want my doll Mollie awful much."

"Then we'll look for her," Freddie said. "Whoa, Whisker!"

Whether the goat really stopped because Freddie said this word, which always makes horses stop, or whether Whisker was tired and wanted a rest, I cannot say. Anyhow, he stopped in a shady place in the woods, and the children got out.

"I'll tie the goat to a tree so he can't go off and have a ride by himself," said Freddie, as he took the strap from the cart.

But Whisker did not seem to want to go on any farther. He lay down on some soft moss and seemed to go to sleep.

"We'll leave him here until we come back," said Freddie. "And we'll look for Helen's doll."

Perhaps the children had an idea that the gypsies may have left the talking doll behind in the woods when they were driven away by the police. For, though they were not near the place where the gypsy men and women had camped, Flossie, Freddie, and Helen began looking under trees and bushes for a trace of the missing Mollie.

"Do you s'pose she can talk and tell you where

she is?" asked Flossie, when they had hunted about a bit, not going too far from the goat-cart.

"I don't know," Helen answered. "Sometimes, when I wind up the spring in her back she says 'Mamma' and 'Papa' without my pushing the button. My father says that's because something is the matter with her."

"Well, if she would only talk now, and call out, we'd know where to look for her," added Freddie.

"Let's call to her," suggested Flossie.

"All right," agreed Helen.

So the children called:

"Mollie! Mollie! Where are you?"

Their voices echoed through the trees, but there was no answer—at least for a while. Then, when they had walked on a little farther, and found a spring of water where they had a cool drink, they called again:

"Mollie! Mollie! Where are you?"

Then, all at once, seemingly from a long way off, came an answering call: "Wait a minute. I'm coming!"

"Oh, did you hear that?" gasped Flossie.

"It was somebody talking to us," whispered Helen.

"And it wasn't the echo, either," said Flossie.

"Maybe it was your doll," suggested Freddie. "Did it sound like her voice?"

"A—a little," said Helen slowly.

"We'll call again," suggested Flossie, and once more the children cried aloud:

"Mollie! Mollie! Where are you?"

"Wait a minute. Stand still so I can find you! I'm coming!" was the answer.

The three little ones looked at one another in surprise, and they were, moreover, a little frightened. Was it possible that the missing talking doll was really in the woods and had answered them? That it could talk, because it had a gramophone inside, they all knew. But would it answer when spoken to?

"It didn't sound like Mollie," whispered Helen, after a bit. "Her voice wasn't as loud as that."

"Oh-o-o-o-o!" Flossie suddenly gasped. "Maybe it was—the gypsies!"

That was something the children had not thought of before. Suppose it should be the same gypsy man who had taken away the doll?

"It couldn't be the gypsies," said Freddie, looking around him. "They all went away."

"But maybe there was *one* left," suggested his sister.

"Pooh! I'm not afraid of *one* gypsy," declared Freddie. "If he bothers me I'll set Whisker on him."

"You can't set a goat—they can't bite or bark like a dog," retorted Flossie.

"No, but Whisker can butt with his horns!" cried Freddie. "That's what I'll do! If it's a gypsy I'll set Whisker on him!"

Just then the children heard the voice again, calling:

"Where are you?"

Once more they looked at one another rather

afraid. And then came a loud "Baa-a-a-a-a!" from Whisker.

"Come on!" cried Freddie. "Maybe they're trying to take our goat away!"

He started on a run through the woods towards the place where they had left Whisker and the goat-cart, now out of sight behind some bushes.

"Wait! Wait for me!" cried Flossie, who was left behind with Helen. "Don't run off without us, Freddie!"

"Oh, excuse me," he said, politely enough. "But we don't want those gypsies to take Whisker."

"Whisker'll butt 'em," said Flossie. "Wait for us."

"Yes, I guess our goat won't let anybody take him," said Freddie, walking now, instead of running. "Come on, Flossie and Helen! Maybe it's your doll talking and maybe it isn't. But we'll soon see!"

Together the three children hurried on, soon coming within sight of the goat. There was Whisker peacefully lying down, still asleep. And running towards him, along the woodland path, was Bert, who, as he caught sight of Freddie and the others, called:

"Oh, there you are! I've been looking everywhere for you. Didn't you hear me calling?"

"Was that you?" asked Freddie. "We thought maybe it was a gypsy man."

"Or Helen's doll," added Flossie. "Her doll, Mollie, can talk, you know, Bert. And Whisker gave us a ride here so we looked for the doll."

"Yes, and then I had to come looking for you," said her brother. "But never mind. I've found you and I've got jolly news."

"Do you mean jolly news because you found us?" asked Freddie.

"No, it's jolly news about something else," Bert said. "But I've got to hurry home with you so Mother won't worry. Then I'll tell you."

CHAPTER VII

"WHERE IS SNAP?"

"HOW did you kids come to run away?" asked Bert, when he was driving the goat-cart back through the woods again, taking a path that was not quite so bumpy as the first one. "My goodness! I came back from Dad's office to find Mother and Nan looking everywhere for you. How did you happen to run away?"

"We didn't runned away," said Flossie, who was so excited over what had happened that she forgot to speak the way her teacher in school had told her to. "Whisker runned away with us."

"I guess he didn't go without being told, and without someone's taking off his hitching strap," said Bert, with a smile.

"Anyhow, we didn't run much, Whisker just walked most of the time," said Freddie.

"Well, it's all the same," returned Bert. "I had to chase after you to find you. Anyhow, you mustn't come off to the woods alone, you kids."

"We had Whisker with us," Freddie declared. "And if any of the gypsy men had come he'd have butted 'em with his horns, wouldn't he?"

"He might, and he might not," said Bert. "Anyhow, I guess you had a nice ride."

"We did," said Flossie. "Only we're sorry we couldn't find Helen's doll. How did you find us, Bert?"

"Oh, I could see by the wheel and hoof marks in the soft dirt which way Whisker had taken you, and I just followed."

"But what is the jolly news?" Freddie demanded. "Are we going back to New York?"

"Better than that!" answered Bert. "We're going camping!"

"Camping?" cried the two little Bobbsey twins in the same breath. "Where?" asked Freddie. "When?" asked Flossie.

"It isn't all settled yet," answered Bert. "You know Dad and Mother talked about it when we were in the big city. And today, when I was down at the lumber-yard I heard Dad speaking to a man in there about some of the islands in Lake Metoka. Dad wanted to know which one was the best to camp on."

"And did the man say which was a good one?" asked Freddie.

"I didn't hear. But I asked Dad afterwards if we were going to camp this summer, and he said he guessed so, if Mother wanted to."

"Does Mother want to?" asked Flossie eagerly.

"She says she does," answered Bert. "So I guess we'll go to camp this summer all right. Isn't that jolly news?"

"Wonderful!" cried Freddie.

"Oh, I wish we could go now and take Whisker with us!" cried Flossie.

"If we go we'll take the goat-cart!" decided Bert.

"And we'll take our dog Snap, and our cat Snoop, too!" announced Freddie. "They'll like to go camping."

Mrs. Bobbsey and Nan were anxiously waiting for Bert to come back with the runaways. When he came in sight, driving the goat-cart, the children's mother hurried down the road to meet them.

"Oh, my dears! You shouldn't go away like that!" she called.

"Whisker wanted to go," said Freddie. "And we had a nice ride even if it was bumpy. And we thought we heard Helen's doll calling, but it was Bert."

"Well, don't do it again," said Mrs. Bobbsey. She always said that, whenever either set of twins did things they ought not to do, and each time they promised to mind. But the trouble was they hardly ever did the same thing twice. And as there were so many things to do, Mrs. Bobbsey could not think of them all.

"When are we going camping?" asked Freddie, as he got out of the goat-cart.

"And which island are we going to?" asked Flossie.

"Oh, my! I see you have it all settled so soon!" laughed Mrs. Bobbsey. "Your father and I have yet to talk it over."

"We'll do that tonight," she went on. "And now you children come in and get washed, and Dinah will give you something to eat. You must be hungry."

"We are," said Flossie. "And Helen's hungry, too. Aren't you, Helen?" she asked.

"Um—yes—I guess so."

"Well, we'll soon find out," laughed Mrs. Bobbsey. "I think your mother won't mind if I give you a little lunch with Flossie and Freddie. Nan can tell her that you are here and are all right. She doesn't know you had a runaway ride in the goat-cart."

And while Flossie, Freddie, and Helen ate the nice little lunch Dinah got ready for them, Bert and Nan went for a ride in the goat-cart, stopping at Mrs. Porter's house to tell her that Helen was safe in the Bobbsey home.

"And now let's talk about camping!" cried Bert that night after supper when the family, twins included, were gathered in the dining-room, the table having been cleared. "When can we go?"

"I think as soon as school closes," said his father. "Summer seems to have started early this year, and I want to get you children and your mother off to some cool place. An island in the middle of the lake is the best place I know of."

"It will be fine!" cried Bert. "Which island are we going to camp on?"

"There are two or three that would do nicely," answered Mr. Bobbsey. "I talked to some friends who own them, but I think one called Blueberry Island would suit us best."

"It has a nice name," said Nan. "I like it—

Blueberry Island! It sounds just as if it were out of a book."

"Is it a fairy island?" Freddie wanted to know, for he liked to have fairy stories read to him.

"Well, maybe it will turn out to be a fairy story," said Mr. Bobbsey with a laugh. "It's the largest island in the lake, and several other parties are going there camping, so Mr. Ames, the man who owns it, told me."

"Why do they call it Blueberry Island?" asked Mrs. Bobbsey.

"Because there are many blueberries on it," Mr. Bobbsey answered. "And if we go there I shall expect you children to pick plenty of blueberries so Dinah can make pies. I'm very fond of blueberry pie."

"I like it, too," said Freddie. "We'll take Whisker with us, and he can haul a whole cart load of blueberries."

"I wouldn't ask you to pick as many as that," said his father with a laugh. "Two or three pounds would be enough for a pie, wouldn't they, Mother?"

"I should hope so! But do you really mean we are to go camping on Blueberry Island?"

"Surely," answered Mr. Bobbsey. "It will be a nice way to spend the summer."

"And shall we live in a tent?" asked Freddie, "and cook over a camp fire? And go fishing?"

"Yes, all of that and more, too," said his father, catching up the little fat fireman and bouncing him towards the ceiling.

Then followed a happy hour talking over the

plans for going camping on Blueberry Island, until Mrs. Bobbsey said it was time for Flossie and Freddie, at least, to go to bed.

Off they went to dream of living in a big white tent with a flag on top of it.

"Just like a circus!" as Freddie said the next morning at breakfast.

"Or a gypsy camp," added Flossie. "Are there any gypsies on Blueberry Island, Daddy?"

"No, not a one."

" 'Cause if there was," went on the little girl, "I wouldn't take my doll with me. I wouldn't want her taken away like Helen's was."

"We won't let any gypsies come," said Mr. Bobbsey.

"And we'll take Whisker, our goat, and Snap and Snoop," said Flossie, "and my dolls and the beetles that go around and around and around and——"

"You'll have a regular menagerie!" said Nan.

"We'll have some fun, anyhow," cried Freddie. "I wonder if we could hitch Snap and Whisker up together and make a team?"

"Let's try," suggested Bert. "Come on, Freddie, we'll find our dog."

But when they called Snap he did not come running in from the garden or barn as he had always done before. Bert and Freddie called, but there was no answering bark.

"Where is Snap, Dinah?" asked Bert, when a search about the house did not reveal the missing dog.

"I saw him here about half an hour ago," said the cook, "an' then, all at once, I didn't see him again. I wonder if that old peddler could have taken him?" she asked, speaking half to herself.

Bert and Freddie looked at one another in surprise. Where was Snap?

CHAPTER VIII

OFF TO CAMP

"THIS is queer," said Bert, when a more careful search about the house and barn failed to find Snap. "If he's run away, it will be the first time he has done that since we've had him."

"Let's ask at some of the houses down the street," said Nan. "Sometimes the children coax him in to play with them, and he forgets to come home because they make such a fuss over him."

"Here's Snoop, anyhow!" cried Freddie, coming out of the barn with the big black cat in his arms. "He can go to camp with us."

"But we want Snap, too!" added Flossie. "We need a dog to keep the gypsies away."

"There won't be any gypsies on Blueberry Island!" Bert reminded them.

"Maybe there'll be one or two, an' I don't want them to take my doll the way they did Helen's," said Flossie.

"Didn't Helen get her doll back?" asked Mrs. Bobbsey, coming out of the house in time to hear what the children were saying.

"No, Mother, and she feels awful sad," replied Flossie. "And now the gypsies has took Snap."

"The gypsies have *taken* Snap—really, Flossie, you must speak more correctly," said Mrs. Bobbsey. "But what do you mean about Snap's being taken?"

"He seems to be gone," reported Bert.

"We've looked everywhere for him, and now we're going to ask down the street," added Nan.

"But we've got Snoop," said Flossie, and so it was. "We"—that is, she and Freddie both—had the big black cat, one twin carrying the head and the other twin the hind legs. But Snoop was often carried that way and he did not mind.

"Snap not here? That is odd," said Mrs. Bobbsey. "Have you whistled and called to him?"

"Every way we know," replied Bert. "Listen!" and, putting his fingers in his mouth, he gave such a shrill whistle that his Mother and Nan had to cover their ears, while Dinah, looking out of her kitchen window, cried:

"Good land of mercy! What is that—a fire whistle?"

"I can whistle like that!" shouted Freddie, dropping his end of the black cat. As it happened to be the head end he was carrying, this left the hind legs to Flossie and poor Snoop was dangling head down.

"Miaou!" he cried sadly, and then he gave a wriggle, and another one, and got loose.

Freddie made a sort of hissing sound on his fingers—not at all a nice, loud whistle as Bert had done—but it was pretty good for a little fellow.

"He ought to hear that," Bert said, when he had finished whistling, and his mother and sister had uncovered their ears. "But he doesn't come."

"Did you ask Dinah about him?" Mrs. Bobbsey questioned.

"Yes, and she said—— Oh, she said something about a peddler!" cried Nan. "We forgot to ask her what she meant."

"Did Snap chase after a peddler?" asked Bert, for the cook was still at the window.

"No. I didn't see your dog chase after the peddler, honey lamb," replied Dinah. "But just a little while ago a woman with a red dress on, all trimmed with yellow, real fancy like, came to the back door selling lace work. Snap was here then, eating some scraps I put out for him, an' the woman patted him an' talked to him in a strange way."

"She did!" cried Bert excitedly. "What'd she say?"

"Land of goodness! You don't s'pose I know all the queer languages in the United States, do you, Bert?" asked Dinah, shaking her head. "But the woman talked queer to Snap, an' he wagged his tail, which he doesn't often do to strangers."

"No," put in Flossie, shaking her head vigorously, "Snap doesn't often talk to strangers. He's awful dig—dignified with 'em. Isn't he, Freddie?"

"Well, he doesn't like tramps, and they're strangers," replied her brother. "Are peddlers tramps, Bert?"

"No, I guess not. But some of 'em look like tramps—pretty near, maybe."

"What happened to the woman peddler?" asked Mrs. Bobbsey.

"Oh, I soon got rid of her," said Dinah. "I told her we were going to live in the woods an' we didn't want any fancy lace 'cause it would get all ripped on the trees an' bushes. So she went off."

"And what happened to Snap?" asked Mrs. Bobbsey.

"Oh, he was eating his scraps the last I saw of him," answered Dinah. "An' he wagged his tail again at the woman in the gay dress which looked like she was going on a picnic."

"A dress of red and yellow," said Nan. "Aren't they the colours the gypsies wear?"

"Was the woman a gypsy?" asked Bert quickly.

"She might have been," answered the cook. "She had gold rings in her ears. I didn't pay too much attention to her, 'cause I was making a cake. But maybe Snap followed her to see to it that she didn't take anything. 'Cause if she was a gypsy she might take things."

"Yes, and she's taken Snap—that's what she's done!" cried Bert. "That's what's happened to our dog. The gypsies have him! I'm going to tell Dad, and have him get a policeman."

"Now don't be too sure," advised Mrs. Bobbsey. "Perhaps that peddler may have been a gypsy, and she may have made friends with Snap—those people have a strange way with them about dogs and horses—but it isn't fair to say she took your pet. He may have followed her just to be friendly. You had better ask at some of the houses down the street first."

"Come on!" cried Bert to Nan. "We'll go and ask."

"And I'm coming, too!" added Freddie. "I can call Snap and you can whistle for him, Bert."

"And I'll take Snoop, and Snoop can miaou for him," said Flossie.

"No, you two little ones stay here," directed Mrs. Bobbsey. "I want to wash and dress you for dinner. Let Bert and Nan hunt for Snap."

So while Flossie and Freddie went into the house to get freshened up after their play, Nan and Bert went from house to house asking about Snap. But though the big trick dog sometimes went to play with the neighbours' children, this time there was no sign of him. One after another of the families, living near by, said they had not seen Snap.

Several persons had noticed the gypsy woman "peddler," as they called her, for she had made a number of calls in the neighbourhood, trying to sell her lace, but no one had seen Snap with her.

"Oh, I guess Snap just ran away for a change, as Flossie and Freddie sometimes do," said Mr. Bobbsey when he came home that evening and had been told what had happened. "He'll come back all right, I'm sure."

But Nan and Bert were not so sure of this. They knew Snap too well. He had never gone away like this before. Flossie and Freddie, being younger, did not worry so much. Besides, they had Snoop, and the cat was more their pet than was the dog, who was Bert's favourite, though, of course, everyone in the Bobbsey family loved him.

Several times that evening Bert went outside to whistle and call for his pet, but there was no answering bark, and when bedtime came Bert was so worried that Mr. Bobbsey agreed to call the police and ask the officers who were on night duty to keep a lookout for the missing animal. This would be done, the chief said, since nearly all the officers in Lakeport knew Snap, who often visited the police station.

Morning came, but no Snap was at the door waiting to be let in, though Bert was up early to look. Snoop, the big black cat, was in his usual place, getting up to stretch and rub against Bert's legs.

"But where's Snap?" asked the boy.

"Miaou," was all Snoop answered.

"Well, I'm afraid your dog is lost," said Mr. Bobbsey, when at the breakfast table Bert reported that Snap was still away. "We'll put an advertisement in the paper and offer a reward if he is brought back."

"Maybe he's gone to camp on Blueberry Island and is waiting over there for us," said Flossie.

"Maybe, my little fat fairy!" agreed her father, catching her up for a good-bye kiss. "Let's hope so. And now you must soon begin to get ready to go camping."

The children heard this news with delight, and, for a time, even lost Snap was forgotten. He had often visited the neighbours before, and had always come back, so Bert hoped the same thing would happen this time.

There was much to do to get ready to go to Blueberry Island. There were clothes to pack and food to be bought, for though it was not many miles from the island back to the mainland where there were stores, still Mrs. Bobbsey did not want to have to send in too often for what was needed.

The goat-cart was very useful for going on errands during the days that it took them to get ready to go off to live in the woods. Bert and Nan, sometimes with Flossie and Freddie, rode here and there about town, and Whisker was as good as a pony, being strong and gentle.

Everywhere they went, Nan and her brother looked for Snap and asked about him. But though many in Lakeport knew the dog, and had seen him on the day he was last noticed, no one could tell where he was. No one could be found who had seen him with the gypsy woman—if he had gone with her—though a number said they had noticed the gaudy, red-and-yellow-dressed peddler strolling about with her lace.

"Our dog's gone and Helen's doll is gone," said Nan the night before they were to go to camp. "I wonder what will be taken next?"

"I hope they don't get our Snoop," said Flossie, as she went to look at the big black cat who was sleeping in the box with a handle, in which he was to be taken to the island.

"And I hope they let Whisker alone," said Freddie.

"Whisker can take care of himself, with his horns," observed Bert. "I'm not afraid of a gypsy trying to get our goat."

The tents had been sent to the island, and a man would set them up. Plenty of good things to eat were packed in boxes and baskets. Dinah and Sam had made ready to go to camp, for they were included in the family. Dinah was to do the cooking and her husband was to look after the boats and firewood.

"And, oh, what fun we'll have!" cried Flossie the next morning, when the sun rose warm and bright and they started for Blueberry Island.

"It would be better if we had Snap," said Bert. "You don't know how I miss that dog!"

"We all do," said Mrs. Bobbsey. "Perhaps we'll find him when we come back, Bert. Your father will come back from the island once or twice a week, and he'll come to the house to see if Snap has come back."

"He'll never come back," said Bert, with a sad face. "I'm sure the gypsies took him, and they'll keep him when they find out he can do circus tricks."

"Well, maybe we'll find the gypsies and, if they have Snap, we can make them give him up," said Nan.

"I hope so," murmured Bert.

There was a small steamer that made trips across the lake, and in this the Bobbseys were to go to Blueberry Island, as they had so many things to take with them that a small boat would never have held them all.

CHAPTER IX

A NIGHT SCARE

"WELL, are you all ready?" asked Mr. Bobbsey, as he came out and locked the front door. On the steps in front of him, or else down the front path, were Mrs. Bobbsey, Nan, Bert, Flossie, Freddie, Sam, Dinah, Snoop, in his travelling crate, Whisker, the goat, hitched to his cart, and a pile of trunks, boxes, and other things.

"If we're not ready we never will be," said Mrs. Bobbsey with a sigh and a laugh, as she looked over everything. "We aren't going so far that we cannot send for anything we forget, which is a good thing. But I guess we're all ready, Daddy."

"Good! Here comes the carter for our trunks, and behind him is the taxi we're going to take down to the steamer dock. Now have you children everything you want?" and he looked at Flossie and Freddie particularly.

"I've got my best doll, and Snoop's in his cage," said Flossie. "And my other dolls are in the trunk and so are the toys I want. Is your fire engine packed, Freddie? 'Cause you might want it if the woods got on fire."

"Yes; my fire engine is all right," answered the little fellow. "An' I've got everything I want, I

guess except—maybe——" he was thinking then.
"Oh, I forgot 'em! I forgot 'em!" he quickly cried.
"Open the door, Daddy! I forgot 'em!"

"Forgot what?" his father asked with a smile.

"The tin beetles that go around and around and
around," answered Freddie. "You know, the ones
I bought in New York. I want 'em."

"Well, it's a good thing you thought of them
before we got away, for I wouldn't have wanted to
come back just to get the tin beetles."

"But they go around and around and around!"
cried Flossie, who liked the queer toys as much as
did her brother. "They're lots of fun."

"Well, as long as we're going to camp on Blueberry Island for fun as much as for anything else,"
said Mr. Bobbsey, "I suppose we'll have to get the
beetles. Come on, Freddie."

The little twin had wrapped his tin beetles in a
paper and left them on a chair in the front hall, so
it was little trouble to get them. Then the trunks,
bags, and bundles were piled in the truck and taken
to the steamboat dock, while the Bobbsey family,
all except Bert, took their places in the taxi. Bert
was to drive Whisker to the wharf, as it was found
easier to ship the goat and goat-cart this way than
by crating or boxing the animal and his cart.

"I'd rather ride with Bert and Whisker than in
the taxi," said Freddie wistfully, as he saw his
brother about to drive off.

"So would I!" added Flossie, who always chimed
in with anything her twin brother did.

"But you can't," said Mrs. Bobbsey decidedly.

"If you two small twins went with Bert in the goat-cart something would be sure to happen. You'd stop to give someone a ride or you'd have a race with a dog or a cat, and then we'd miss the boat. You must come with us, Flossie and Freddie, and, Bert, don't lose any time. The boat won't wait for you and Whisker."

"I'll be there before you," promised Bert, and he was, for he took a short cut. He said on the way he had stopped at the police station to ask if there was any news about the missing Snap, but the trick dog had not been seen, and so the Bobbseys went to camp without him.

If there had not been so much to see and to do, they would have been more lonesome for Snap than they were. As it was, they missed him very much, but Bert held out a little hope by saying perhaps they might find their pet on Blueberry Island, though why he said it he hardly knew.

"All aboard!" called the steamboat men as the Bobbseys settled themselves in comfort, their luggage having been put in place. The goat-cart was left on the lower deck where the cars stood that were to be taken across the lake, for the steamer was a sort of ferryboat. "All aboard!" called the deck hands.

There was a tooting of whistles, a clanging and ringing of bells, and the boat slowly moved away from the dock.

"Oh, it's just lovely to go camping!" sighed Nan.

"We haven't really begun yet," said Bert. "Wait

until we get to the woods and have to go hunting for what we want to eat, and cook it over an open fire—that's the way to live!"

"I guess there won't be much hunting on Blueberry Island," said Mr. Bobbsey, with a laugh.

"Well, we can make-believe, can't we?" asked Freddie.

"Oh, yes, you can make-believe," said his mother. "And that, sometimes, is more fun than having real things."

I shall not tell you all the things that happened on the steamboat, for so much more happened on Blueberry Island that I shall have to hurry on to that. Besides, the trip to the middle of the lake did not take more than an hour, and not much can take place in an hour.

I say not much, and yet sometimes lots of things can. But not a great deal did to the Bobbseys this time, though, to be sure, a strange dog tried to get hold of Snoop in his crate, and Freddie nearly fell overboard reaching after his hat, which blew off.

"But I could swim even if I did fall in," he said, for Mr. Bobbsey had taught all four twins how to keep afloat in water.

"Well, we don't want you falling in," his mother answered. "Now you sit by me."

This Freddie did for a short time. Then he got tired of sitting still and jumped down from his chair, at the same time calling to his little sister:

"Say, Flossie, let's go and watch the engine."

"All right," answered the little girl, ready, as always, to do anything her brother suggested.

As Flossie jumped from her chair to join her brother, she accidentally kicked an umbrella belonging to a man who was sitting near by, and the umbrella fell to the floor and slipped out under the railing right into the water.

"Oh—oh—oh!" gasped Flossie.

But Freddie turned and ran as fast as he could to the stairs that led to the lower deck.

"Here! where are you going?" cried his father, and started after his son.

"Goin' after that umbrella!"

"I think not!" and Mr. Bobbsey caught up with Freddie and picked him up in his arms.

Meanwhile, Mrs. Bobbsey told the man how sorry she was, and that they would replace the umbrella. But the man insisted that he would not allow that.

"No one needs an umbrella on such a lovely day, anyway," he said.

But a deck hand who was cleaning some mops in the water had already rescued the umbrella.

"Blueberry Island!" called a man on the steamer, after the boat had made one or two other stops. "All off for Blueberry Island!"

"Oh, let us off! Let us off!" cried Flossie, getting up in such a hurry from her deck chair that she dropped her doll. "We're going camping there."

"I guess the passengers know it by this time, without your telling them," laughed her father. "'But come on—don't forget anything."

Such a scrambling as there was! Such a gathering together of packages—umbrellas—fishing rods—

hats, caps, gloves, and the crate with black Snoop in it. Sam and Dinah helped all they could, and between them and Mr. and Mrs. Bobbsey and the children the family managed to get ashore at last.

A gangplank had been run from the boat to the dock, and over this Bert drove Whisker and the goat-cart. The goat seemed glad to get off the steamboat.

"Oh, wouldn't Snap just love it here!" cried Nan, as they went on shore and looked at the island. "Isn't it too bad he isn't with us?"

"I'm going to find him!" declared Bert. "Those old gypsies shan't have our trick dog!"

Blueberry Island was, indeed, a fine place for a camp. In the winter no one lived on it, but in the summer it was often visited by picnic parties and by those who liked to gather the blueberries which grew so plentifully, giving the island its name.

In fact, so many people came to one end of the island in the berry season that a man had set up a little stand near the shore, where he sold sandwiches, coffee, sweets, and ice cream, since many of the berry pickers, and others who came, grew hungry after tramping through the woods.

But where Mr. Bobbsey was going to camp with his family, the berry pickers and picnic parties seldom came, as it was on the far end of the island, so our friends would be rather by themselves, which was what they wanted.

Mr. Dalton, the man who kept the little refreshment stand, had his horse and wagon on the island, and he had agreed to haul the Bobbseys' trunks and other things to where their tents, already put up, awaited them.

"And can't we ride there in the goat-cart?" asked Freddie of his mother, as he saw Bert get up behind Whisker in the little cart.

"Yes, I think you and Flossie may ride now that we are on the island," said Mrs. Bobbsey. "Do you want to go, Nan?"

"No, I'll walk with you and Daddy. I'll get enough goat rides later."

"Oh, how nice it is!" cried Mrs. Bobbsey when she and Nan came in sight of the tents of the camp. "I know we shall like it here!"

"I hope you will," said Mr. Bobbsey. "And now we must see about something to eat. I suppose the children are hungry."

"They're always that way!" laughed Dinah. "I never saw 'em when they weren't hungry. But just show me where the cook-stove is an' something to cook, an' they won't be hungry long, my honey lambs!"

Dinah was as good as her word, and she soon had a fine meal on the table in the dining-tent, for the men Mr. Bobbsey had hired to set up the canvas houses had everything in readiness to go right to "housekeeping", as Nan said.

There were several tents for the Bobbsey family. One large one was for the family to sleep in, while a smaller one, near the kitchen tent, was for Dinah and her husband. Then there was a tent that served as a dining-room, and another where the trunks and food could be stored. In this tent was an ice-box, for a boat stopped at the island every day and left a supply of ice.

The children helped to unpack and set up camp, though, if the truth were told, perhaps they did more to upset it than otherwise. But Mr. and Mrs. Bobbsey were used to this, and knew how to manage.

So the meal was eaten, Whisker was put in his little stable, made under a pile of brushwood, and the children went out rowing in a boat. They had lots of fun that afternoon, and Bert even did a little hunting for Snap, thinking that, by some chance, the trick dog might be on the island. But Snap was not to be found.

"Though, of course, we didn't half look," Bert said. "We'll look again tomorrow."

And now it was evening in "Twin Camp", as the Bobbseys had decided to call their place on Blueberry Island. There had been quite a talk as to what to name the camp, but when Dinah suggested "Twin", everyone agreed that it was best. So "Twin Camp" it was called, and Daddy Bobbsey said he would have a wooden sign made with that on it, and a flag to hoist over it on a pole.

Beds were made up in the sleeping tent, and soon even Nan and Bert declared that they were ready to go to bed. They had been up early and had been very busy. Flossie and Freddie dropped off to sleep as soon as they put their heads on the pillows.

Freddie did not know what time it was when he awakened. It was in the night, he was sure of that, for it was dark in the tent except where the little lantern was aglow. What had awakened him was something bumping against him. His cot was near one of the walls of the sleeping tent and he awoke with a start.

"Hi!" he called, as he felt something strike against him. "Who's doing that? Stop it! Stop it, I say!"

"Freddie, are you talking in your sleep?" asked his mother, who had not slept very soundly.

"No, I'm not asleep," Freddie answered. "But something bumped me. It's outside the tent."

"Maybe it's Whisker feeling for you with his horns," said Flossie, who slept near her brother, and who had been awakened when he called out so loudly.

"It—it didn't feel like Whisker. It was softer than his horns," Freddie said. "Mummy, I want to come into your bed."

"No, Freddie, you must stay where you are. I guess it was only the wind blowing on you."

"No, it wasn't!" said Freddie. "It was a bump that hit me. I'm afraid over here!"

CHAPTER X

THE "GO-AROUND" BEETLES

WITHOUT waiting for his mother to tell him that he might, Freddie slipped off his cot and went scurrying over the board floor of the tent towards Mrs. Bobbsey's bed.

"I'm coming, too!" said Flossie, who generally went everywhere her small brother did.

"Did something hit you, too?" asked Freddie, turning to his sister.

"No, but it might. If you are afraid I'm afraid, too."

"Oh, you children!" said Mrs. Bobbsey with a sigh. "I believe you only dreamed it, Freddie."

"No, Mummy, I didn't! Really I didn't! Something bumped me from outside the tent. It hit me in the back—not hard, but sort of soft like, an'—an' I woke up. I want to sleep with you!"

"What's it all about?" asked Daddy Bobbsey. Then Freddie had to explain again, and Flossie also talked until Nan and Bert were awakened.

"It might have been Whisker," said Bert. "If he got loose and brushed against the tent and Freddie had rolled with his back close against the side it would be like that."

79

Just then there sounded in the night the "Baa-a-a-a-a!" of the white goat.

"There he is!" cried Bert.

"But it sounds as though he were still safely tied up," said Mr. Bobbsey. "I'll have a look outside. Too bad we haven't Snap with us. He'd give the alarm in a minute if anything were wrong."

The goat bleated again, but the sound did not seem near the tent, as it would have done if Whisker had been loose. Putting on his bathrobe and slippers, Mr. Bobbsey took a lantern and went outside. Bert wanted to go with his father, but Mrs. Bobbsey would not hear of it.

"We want a young man in here to look after us," she said, smiling.

"I'm almost a man. I can make my fire engine go," Freddie said, forgetting his fright, now that the "big folks" were up, and the light in the tent was turned higher.

They could hear Mr. Bobbsey walking around outside, and they heard him speaking to the goat, who bleated again. Mr. Bobbsey was as fond of animals as were his children, and Whisker was almost like a dog, he was so tame and gentle.

"Was the goat loose, Daddy?" asked Nan, when her father came back into the tent.

"No, he was tied all right in his little stable. It wasn't Whisker who brushed against Freddie."

"*Something* did!" declared the small boy. "Didn't I wake up?"

"Well, you might have dreamed it," said Nan. "You often talk in your sleep, I know."

"I did feel something bump me," declared Freddie, and nothing the others could say would make him change his idea.

"Did you see anything?" Mrs. Bobbsey asked her husband in a low voice when the twins were in their beds again. Flossie's and Freddie's cots were moved over nearer to those of their parents', and they had dropped off to slumber again, after getting drinks of water.

"Well, I rather think I did," answered Mr. Bobbsey in a low voice.

"You did! What?"

"I don't know whether it was a horse or a man, but it was something. It was so dark I couldn't see well, and the trees and bushes come close to the tents."

"How could it be a horse?"

"It might have been the one that belongs to Mr. Dalton. If the horse were walking around, cropping grass wherever he could find it, he might have brushed past the side of the tent and so have disturbed Freddie."

"Yes, I suppose so," agreed Mrs. Bobbsey. "But couldn't you tell a horse from a man?"

"No, it was too dark. I only just saw a shadow moving away from the tents as I stepped out."

"And was Whisker all right?"

"Yes, though I guess he was lonesome. He tried to follow me back here when I left him."

"I suppose Whisker misses the children," said Mrs. Bobbsey. "But do you think it could be a man who was wandering about our tents?"

"It *could* be—yes."

"One of the gypsies?"

"Oh, I wouldn't say that. In fact, I don't believe the gypsies are anywhere around here. The children have that notion in their heads, but I don't believe in it. Perhaps it was a blueberry picker who was lost."

"But if he was lost, and saw our tents, he'd stop and ask to be set on the right road," went on Mrs. Bobbsey. "Besides, blueberries won't be ripe for another week or so, and nobody picks them green."

"No, I suppose not," agreed Mr. Bobbsey. "Well, I'm sure I don't know who or what it was, but I saw a dark shadow moving away."

"Shadows can't do any harm."

"No, but it takes someone or something to make a shadow, and I'd like to know what it was. I'll take a look around in the morning," said Mr. Bobbsey. "We don't want Twin Camp spoiled by midnight scares."

"Maybe we'd better get another dog, if Snap doesn't come back," suggested Mrs. Bobbsey.

"I'll think about that. We can't very well train Whisker to keep watch. Besides, he can't bark," and Mr. Bobbsey laughed as he got back into bed.

There was no more disturbance that night and the twins did not again awaken. Mr. Bobbsey remained awake for a while, but he heard nothing, and he believed that if it was a man or an animal that had brushed against the tent where Freddie was sleeping, whoever or whatever it was had gone.

Dinah had a fine breakfast ready for the twins and the others the next morning. There were flap-jacks with maple syrup to pour over them, and that, with the crisp smell of bacon, made everyone so hungry that there was no need to call even Nan twice, and sometimes she liked to lie in bed longer than did the others.

"Did you find what it was that bumped me, Daddy?" asked Freddie, as he, at last, pushed back his plate, unable to eat any more.

"No. And we don't need to worry about it. Now we must finish getting Twin Camp in order today," went on Mr. Bobbsey, "and then we will begin to have fun and enjoy ourselves."

"Are we going to catch any fish?" asked Bert. "Always, when you read about campers, they catch fish and fry them."

"Yes, we can go fishing after we get the work done," said his father. "Work first and play after-wards is a rule we'll follow here, though there won't be much work to do. However, if we're to go fishing we'll have to dig some bait."

"I can dig worms!" cried Freddie. "Worms are good for bait, aren't they, Daddy?"

"For some kinds of fish, yes. We'll fish part of the time with worms and see what luck we have. Bert, you and Freddie can dig the bait."

"I want to help," said Flossie. "I helped Nan get out my dolls and toys, and now I want to dig worms."

"All right, little fat fairy!" laughed Bert. "Come along."

"Mercy, Flossie, digging bait is such dirty work! What do you want to do that for?" asked Nan.

"I don't care if it is dirty, it's fun."

"You might have known, Nan," laughed Mrs. Bobbsey, "that Flossie would not object to dirt."

With a shovel for turning up the dirt, and a tin can to hold the worms, Bert and the two smaller twins were soon busy. But they did not have such good luck as they expected. Earthworms were not plentiful on the island. Perhaps they could not swim over the lake from the main shore, Freddie suggested.

"Aren't beetles good for bait?" asked Freddie when he had looked in the tin can and found only a few worms wiggling about after more than half an hour's digging on the part of himself and Bert.

"Some kinds of insects are good for fishing, yes," Bert answered, and, hearing that, Freddie started back for the tent where the trunks were stored.

"What are you going to do?" Bert called after his little brother.

"I'm going to get the go-around bettles. We can use them for bait. Water won't hurt 'em—the store man told me so. We can use the go-around beetles."

"Oh, they're no good—they're *tin*!" laughed Bert.

But Freddie was not listening. He had slipped into the tent and was searching for the toys he had bought in New York. Bert kept on digging for worms, now and then finding one, which Flossie picked up for him, until he heard another call from

Freddie. The little fellow came running from the tent with an empty and broken box in his hand.

"Look! Look!" cried Freddie. "My go-around beetles came to life in the night and they broke out of the box.ᵇ Oh dear! Now I can't have 'em to catch fish with! The go-around beetles broke out of the box and they've gone away!"

CHAPTER XI

THE BLUEBERRY BOY

"WHAT'S the matter, Freddie? What has happened? I hope you haven't hurt yourself," and Mrs. Bobbsey, who heard the small twin calling to Bert about the toys, hurried from the tent, where she was making the beds, to see what the trouble was.

"No, Mummy, I'm not hurt," Freddie answered. "But look at my go-around beetles!" and he held out the empty and broken box.

"What's the matter with them?" asked Mr. Bobbsey, who come up just then from the shore of the lake where he had gone to make sure the camp boats were securely tied.

"My beetles are all gone!" went on Freddie. "They broke out of the box in the night! They bit themselves out!"

"No, they didn't bite the box," said Flossie, coming up to look at what her small brother held. "They just went around and around and around, and they knocked a hole with their heads in the box and so they got out. Did you look for them on the floor of the tent, Freddie?" she asked.

"No, I didn't."

"Come on, we'll have a look," Bert said. He

dropped the shovel with which he had been digging
for worms and ran over to his little brother. He
took the box from Freddie.

"That must have been smashed in the moving,"
Bert said to his father.

"No, it wasn't smashed," Freddie said, hearing
what Bert remarked to Mr. Bobbsey. "Flossie and
I were playing with the beetles yesterday after we
got here, and the box wasn't broken then. It was
all right, and so were the go-around beetles. But
now they're gone!"

"Maybe the box fell off a table or something,"
said Mr. Bobbsey, "and broke that way. We'll look
on the floor of the tent for your beetles, my little
fat fireman."

But no beetles were to be found after a careful
search had been made, and Freddie and Flossie
were quite disappointed.

"We can't go fishing if we can't find any beetles
to bait the hooks," said Freddie, tears in his blue
eyes.

"Never mind," his father answered. "The tin
beetles wouldn't have caught many fish, and if we
don't find your toys I'll get you some more when
I go to town. You and Bert had better keep on
digging for worms, I guess. They're better for
fish."

"And I'll pick 'em up," offered Flossie. She was
a queer little child in some ways, not afraid of
"crawly things".

It did not take Freddie or Flossie long to forget
what had made them unhappy, and though for a

time they were sorry about the loss of the toys, they
soon became so interested in helping Bert dig for
worms that they were quite jolly again.

"Here's an awful fat one, Flossie!" cried Freddie.
"Pick that one up just terribly careful-like. I'm
going to save him for my hook, and maybe I'll get
the biggest fish of all."

"How'll you know where to find this one when
you want it, I'd like to know, Freddie Bobbsey?"
returned his sister.

"Tie a blue ribbon on it," suggested Bert.

"Yes, we might," said Flossie slowly. "Maybe
Nan has a ribbon. I'll ask."

Bert laughed and said, "I was just fooling, little
fat fairy."

Pretty soon Bert dropped the spade he had taken
up and said:

"There, Freddie, you dig awhile. I want to see
about the rods and lines. We have almost worms
enough."

Freddie was glad to do this, and Flossie was
eager to pick up the crawling creatures. Bert went
back to the tent to get out the rods, lines, and
hooks. There he found his father and mother looking at the broken box that had held the tin beetles.

"How do you think it became smashed?" Mrs.
Bobbsey asked.

"I don't know," answered Mr. Bobbsey. "It
looks as though someone had stepped on it."

"But who could do that? Flossie and Freddie
think so much of the toys that they take good care
of them, and they wouldn't put them where they

would be stepped on. Do you suppose any of the men who have been helping set up the camp could have done it?"

"I hardly think so. If they did they wouldn't take the beetles away, and that is what has happened. It seems to me as though the box had been broken so the toys could be taken out. For the cover fits on tightly, and it often sticks. Freddie and Flossie often come to me to open it for them. Probably whoever tried to open it could not do so at first, and then stepped on it enough to crack it open without damaging the tin beetles inside."

"But who would do such a thing?" asked Mrs. Bobbsey, and Bert found himself asking, in his mind, the same question.

"That's something we'll have to find out," said Mr. Bobbsey, and neither of them noticed Bert, who, by this time, was inside the tent where the fishing things were kept.

"Could it be the gypsies?" asked Mrs. Bobbsey.

"Well, I don't altogether believe all that talk about gypsies," said Mr. Bobbsey slowly. "I think they may have taken Helen's talking doll, but that's all. However, if there are any gypsies here on the island, and if they saw those gay red, yellow and spotted beetles of Flossie's and Freddie's they might have taken them. They like those colours, and the little toys might amuse them."

"Oh, but if there are gypsies on this island I don't want to stay camping here! They might take away some of the children—Flossie or Freddie! Nan and Bert are too old."

"Nonsense!" laughed Mr. Bobbsey. "There are no gypsies here, and you needn't worry."

"All the same I wish Snap were here with us," went on Mrs. Bobbsey. "I'd feel safer if I knew the dog were with the children all the while, as he was before."

"Well, if he doesn't come back, or if we don't find him soon, I'll get another dog," promised Mr. Bobbsey. "Now don't worry about gypsies. Maybe this broken box was only an accident."

"But what about the shadow you saw last night? Maybe that was a——"

Just then Dinah came walking from the cook tent towards the large one where Mr. and Mrs. Bobbsey stood.

"Mrs. Bobbsey, did you take that big piece of bacon I cut a few slices from last night?" asked the cook.

"Why, no, Dinah, I didn't," answered Mrs. Bobbsey. "Why do you ask?"

" 'Cause that bacon's gone. It's gone completely! I hung it inside the tent, up high where none of them chatterin' squirrels or chipmunks could get it, an' now when I want some for dinner, it's gone. Maybe the children took some for their fish hooks, 'cause I heard Bert talk about bait."

"No, I didn't take it," answered Bert himself, stepping out of the small tent where the rods, oars for the boats, and other camp articles were kept. "We've got worms enough for bait."

"Bacon gone, eh?" said Mr. Bobbsey. Then, as he looked at his wife and glanced at Bert, he went on: "Well, maybe a stray dog jumped up and got it. Some dogs can jump very high, Dinah. Snap could, I remember."

"Good land of mercy! If I thought that Snap had come back to my honey lambs I'd be so glad that I wouldn't mind the bacon," said Dinah. "But I don't reckon any dog took it, Mr. Bobbsey. I think it was a two-legged robber that——"

"Never mind that now, Dinah!" said Mrs. Bobbsey quickly. "Come here and finish making the beds, I want to walk down to the lake with Mr. Bobbsey," and she nodded to her husband. "One piece of bacon won't matter," she went on.

"Yes, I know *that*," said Dinah, who was puzzled. "But I don't like the idea of thieves coming to our camp——"

"It's time it was stopped, isn't it?" asked Bert, as he walked towards the cook. "Say, Dinah," he went on as he saw his father and mother stroll down to the shore of the lake, "did you hear a queer noise in the night?"

"Did I hear a queer noise around the camp last night?" repeated Dinah. "Well, I sure *did*, honey lamb! I heard an owl hoot, an' that's a sure sign of bad luck."

"No, I don't mean that kind of noise, Dinah. Did you hear anything else?"

"Yes. I heard my man Sam snore something terrible! It was 'most like thunder. Did you-all hear that, honey lamb?"

"No, I didn't hear that, Dinah," answered Bert, with a laugh. "But something or somebody brushed past our tent in the night, and woke up Freddie. Then my father went outside and saw someone sneaking away."

"Oh, my good land of mercy!" cried Dinah. "That's where my bacon went to! Wait until I tell your father, honey lamb, an'——"

"No! Hold on! Wait a minute!" cried Bert, catching Dinah by her apron as she was hurrying away. "Dad knows it already, and so does Mother. I guess they don't want to scare us children, but I'm not afraid. I'll tell you what I think, Dinah."

"What's that?"

"I think there are gypsies on this island, and that they're after Flossie and Freddie!"

"Oh, my goodness! Oh, my goodness! Oh, my goodness!" cried Dinah quickly. It seemed she could think of nothing else to say.

"But I'm not afraid," went on Bert. "We'll just have to keep a good watch, and not let those two little twins out of our sight. Don't tell my mother or father that you know this. You and I and Nan will keep watch."

"That's what we will!" exclaimed the fat cook. "An' if those gypsies lay so much as a fingernail on my honey lambs I'll pull the gold rings off their ears an' throw dish water on 'em—that's what I'll do to those gypsies!"

"I wish we had Snap back, or that Whisker were a dog instead of a goat," said Bert. "But maybe if I let Whisker roam around the camp at night he'll be as good as a watchdog."

"He can butt with his horns," said Dinah.

"Yes, and he can make a bleating noise. That's what I'll do," said Bert. "I'll use Whisker as a watchdog. Now don't say anything to Father or Mother about our knowing there's gypsies here," went on Bert.

"I won't—I won't say a word," promised Dinah. "But I'll keep my old eyes skinned for Flossie an' Freddie, an' so will Sam. It's got to be mighty smart gypsies that'll take away my lambs!"

Bert was really much excited by what he had seen and heard. The smashing of the box, what his father and mother thought about it, the taking of the bacon and the scare the night before—all this was quite a surprise.

"Are you sure it's gypsies?" asked Nan when her elder brother told her what had happened.

"I'm *sure* of it," said Bert. "Now what you and I've got to do is to keep a good watch over Flossie and Freddie. Course we're too big for the gypsies to take, but they could easily walk away with those little twins."

"What d'you s'pose they'd do with 'em, Bert, if they did take Flossie and Freddie?"

"Oh, they wouldn't hurt 'em, of course. They'd just keep 'em until Dad paid a lot of money to get the twins back"

"How much money?"

"Oh, maybe a thousand dollars—maybe more."

"Oh!" exclaimed Nan. "Then we must be sure never to let Flossie or Freddie out of our sight. We've got to watch them every minute."

"Of course," agreed Bert. "We'll fool those gypsies yet."

Carrying out their plan to be very careful of their little brother and sister, Bert and Nan took the small twins in the boat with them when they went fishing an hour later. Bert would not go out far from the shore of Blueberry Island—indeed, his mother had told him he must not, for the lake was deep in places—and the older twins did about as much watching the bushes along the bank for signs of gypsies as they did fishing.

Flossie and Freddie, however, not worrying about any trouble, had lots of fun tossing their baited hooks into the water, and Freddie yelled in delight when he caught the first fish. Flossie also caught one, but it was very small, and Bert made her put it back in the lake.

The children caught enough fish for a meal, though when they started out neither their father nor mother thought they would. But the worms proved to be good bait.

"We'd have caught bigger fish if we'd had my tin beetles for bait," said Freddie.

"I don't want my beetles put on a hook," said Flossie. "When will you find them, Freddie?"

"I don't know," he answered.

The tents were put in good order and for two or three days the children had great sport playing, going fishing and taking walks in the woods with their father and mother, or going for trips on the lake. There were no more night scares.

"Maybe it wasn't gypsies after all," said Nan to her brother one day.

"Yes, it was," he said. "They were here, but they went away when they found out we knew about them. But they'll come back, and then they may try to take Flossie or Freddie. We've got to keep a good watch."

It was about a week after they had come to Blueberry Island that the Bobbsey twins—all four of them—went for a ride in the goat-cart. There was a good road which ran the whole length of the island, and Whisker could easily pull the cart along it.

The twins had taken their lunch and were to have a sort of picnic in the woods. They rode under the green trees, stopped to gather flowers, and Nan made a wreath of ferns which she put over Whisker's horns, making him look very funny indeed. Then the twins found a nice grassy spot near a spring of water, and sat down to eat the good things Dinah had put up for their lunch.

Freddie had taken one bite of a chicken sandwich when, all of a sudden, there was a queer noise in the bushes near him, and a queer face peered out. Freddie gave one look at it, and, dropping his piece of bread and chicken, cried:

"Oh, it's a blueberry boy! It's a blueberry boy! Oh, look!"

CHAPTER XII

THE DRIFTING BOAT

AT first Nan and Bert did not know whether Freddie was playing some trick or not. Flossie had gone down to the spring to get a cupful of water, and so was not near her little brother when he gave the cry of alarm.

But Bert looked up and had a glimpse of what had startled Freddie. Certainly there was a queer, blue face staring at the three twins from over the top of the bushes. And the face did not go away as they looked at it.

"A blueberry boy! What in the world is a blueberry boy?" asked Nan.

"There he is!" cried Freddie, pointing. "He's been picking blueberries. That's why I call him a blueberry boy."

"Yes, and he's been eating them, too, I guess," added Bert. "Did you want anything of us?" he asked the stranger.

By this time Flossie had come back with the water—that is, what she had not spilled of it—and she, too, saw the strange boy.

"Who are you?" she asked.

"My name's Tom," was the answer. "What's yours?"

"Flossie Bobbsey, and I'm a twin and we're camping on this island, and we had some beetles that went around and around and——"

"Flossie, come here," called Nan. She did not want her little sister to talk too much to the strange boy. Nan had an idea the boy might belong to the gypsies.

"I saw him first," put in Freddie. "I saw his face all covered with blueberries, and I dropped my standwich—I did."

He began looking on the ground for what he had been eating, but finding, when he picked up the bread and bits of chicken, that ants were crawling all over the "standwich", he tossed it away again.

"Aw, what'd you do that for?" asked Tom. "That was good to eat! Aren't you hungry?"

"Yes, but I don't like ants," returned Freddie. "'Sides, there's more to eat in the basket!"

"Jeepers!" exclaimed Tom. "That's fine! There isn't anything in *my* basket but blueberries, and not many of them. You get tired of eating 'em after a while, too."

"Are you—are you hungry?" asked Bert. As yet no one else had appeared except the boy. He seemed to be all alone. And he was not much larger than Bert.

"Hungry? I'll tell the world I'm hungry!" answered the boy with a laugh that showed his white teeth with his blueberry-stained lips and face all around them. "I thought I'd have a lot of berries picked by noon, so I could row back to shore, sell 'em and get something to eat. But the berries aren't as ripe as I thought they'd be—it's too early, I guess—so I've got to go hungry."

Nan whispered something to Bert, who nodded.

"We've got more sandwiches here," Bert said to the blueberry boy. "Would you like one?"

"Would I *like* one?" asked the boy, who seemed to answer one question by asking another like it. "Say, you just give me a chance. I haven't had nothing since breakfast, and there wasn't much of that."

With a bound he jumped through the bushes and stood in the little grassy glade where the Bobbsey twins were having a sort of picnic by themselves. They saw that Tom had on ragged clothes and no shoes. Indeed, he looked like a very poor boy, but his face, though it was stained with the blueberries he had eaten, was smiling and kind. The Bobbsey twins thought they would like him.

"Here—eat this," and Bert held out some sandwiches. Dinah had put in plenty, as always.

"And he can have some cake, too," said Freddie. "I don't want but two pieces, and I told Dinah to put in three for me."

"Oh, what a hungry boy!" laughed Nan.

"And the blueberry boy can have one of my pieces of cake," said Flossie. "Where did you get the blueberries?" she asked, looking into his basket.

"I didn't get many—that's the trouble," he said. "It's a little too early for them. But the earlier they are the better price you can sell 'em for. So I came over alone today."

"Where do you live?" asked Bert, as the boy was hungrily eating the sandwich.

"Over in Freedon," and Tom Turner, for such he said was his name, pointed to a village on the other side of the lake from that where the Bobbsey twins had their home. "Our folks come here every year to pick blueberries, but never as early as this. I guess I've had my trouble for nothing. I've eaten more berries than I put in my basket, I guess. But I was so hungry I had to have something. I didn't find many ripe ones at that, and I guess I got as much outside of me as I did inside," and he laughed again, showing his white teeth.

"Where do you folks live?" Tom asked, as he took a piece of cake Nan offered him.

"We're camping on this island."

"You don't mean to say you are gypsies, do you?" asked the blueberry boy in surprise.

"No, of course not!" Bert answered. "We live in Lakeport—Bobbsey is our name and——"

"Oh, does your father have a lumber-yard?"

"Yes."

"Oh! Well, then you're all right! My father drives one of your father's trucks. He just got that job this week—been out of work a long while. I heard him say he had a place in the Bobbsey lumber-yard, but I never thought I'd meet you. I thought maybe you were gypsies at first."

"That's what I thought you were," said Nan.

"We're going to be gypsies when we get older —Freddie and me," announced Flossie.

"No, we're not, Flossie. We're going to be in a circus."

"Oh, yes! And I'm going to ride a horse standing up."

"And I'm going to be a clown——"

"And he'll have his little fire engine——"

"And squirt water on the other clowns and——"

"And the folks'll shout and laugh. And I'm going to have a glittery——"

"Dear me, Flossie and Freddie, we've heard all about that at least a dozen times lately," protested Bert.

"But Tom hasn't heard about it. He's interested," declared Freddie.

"I knew a feller once that had been in a circus," said Tom. "He said they had to work awful hard. There's the show every afternoon and every night and the parade in the morning and the practising and getting ready. He said too that the fellers at the head of the show was awful strict about how everybody behaved themselves. It wasn't much fun, he said, and it was lots of work."

"My!" gasped Freddie. "I—I guess we'll be gypsies. I don't like to work—much."

"That is, not very much," agreed Flossie.

"Are there any gypsies here?" asked Bert, for he thought it would be a good chance to find out what he wanted to know.

"Yes, there are some," was Tom's unexpected answer. "They had a camp on the lower end of the island last week. I expected to see some of 'em today. They're great blueberry pickers, and that's one reason I came early. Most always the gypsies get the best of the blueberries 'fore we folks have a chance."

"Are there gypsies on this island now?" asked Nan, looking over her shoulder into the bushes, as though she feared a dark-faced man, with gold rings in his ears, might step out any moment and make a grab for Flossie or Freddie.

"Well, I guess they're here now, 'less they've gone," said Tom. "I saw some of the men and women here day before yesterday. They had been over to the mainland buyin' things from the store, and they rowed over here. I'd come to look for blueberries, but there weren't as many ripe as there are today, though that isn't saying much. But the gypsies are here all right."

"Then we'd better go," said Nan to Bert.

"Why?" Tom asked.

"Because," said Nan slowly, "we don't like gypsies. They might take——"

"They took Helen's talking doll!" exclaimed Flossie. "She cried about it, too. I would if they'd taken my doll, only I have her hidden under my bed. You won't tell the gypsies, will you?"

"No, indeed!" laughed Tom. "You're afraid of them, are you?" he asked Nan.

"Yes—a little," she said slowly.

"They won't hurt you!" Tom said. "They're not very fond of working, and they'll take anything they find lying around loose, but they won't hurt anybody."

"They took Helen's doll," said Freddie, who had finished his two pieces of cake, "and maybe they got my toy beetles that go around and around——"

"And around! They go around three times," put in Flossie.

"I was going to say that, only you didn't wait!" cried Freddie. "But we've got a goat!" he went on, "and he's almost as good as Snap, our dog, and maybe the gypsies got him."

"My, you don't think of anything but gypsies!" said Tom with a laugh. "I'm not worried about them. If I see any of 'em on the island I'll ask 'em if they have your dog and beetles."

"And Helen's doll," added Flossie. "She wants Mollie back."

"I'll ask about that," promised Tom. "You've been awful good to me, and I'd like to do you a favour. I know some of the gypsy boys."

"I guess I'll tell my father they're camping on this island," said Bert.

"Let's go tell him now," suggested Nan. "We've stayed here long enough."

"And I guess I'll row back to the mainland," added Tom. "There's no use waiting here for the blueberries to get ripe. I'll come next week."

He walked back a little way with the Bobbsey twins to where he had left his boat. Then he was soon rowing across the lake, waving his hand to his new friends, his white teeth showing between his berry-stained lips.

"He's a nice boy—that blueberry boy," said Freddie. "I saw him first, I did!"

Mr. Bobbsey nodded his head thoughtfully when the twins told him what Tom had said.

"Gypsies on the island, eh?" remarked Mr. Bobbsey. "Well, I suppose they think they have a right to camp here. But I'll see about it. Maybe some of them are all right, but I don't like the idea of staying here if the place is going to be overrun with them."

For the next few days and nights a close watch was kept about Twin Camp, but no gypsies were seen. Nor did any more blueberry-pickers come. Indeed, the fruit was not ripe enough, as the Bobbseys could tell by looking at some bushes which grew near their tents.

It was about a week after this, when Mr. Bobbsey had gone to Lakeport one morning on business, that Flossie and Freddie went down to the shore of the lake not far from their camp.

As they looked across the water they saw an empty rowboat drifting towards the island. There was no one in it, as they could tell, and the wind was sending it slowly along.

"It's got loose from some dock," said Freddie, who knew more about boats than most boys of his age.

"Maybe it'll come here and we can get it," said Flossie. "Let's throw stones at it."

"No, that would only scare it away," said Freddie. "Wait till it gets near enough, and then I'll wade out and poke it in with a stick."

So the two little twins waited on shore for the drifting boat to come to them.

CHAPTER XIII

IN THE CAVE

"LOOK out, Freddie! Don't you go wading too far!" cried Flossie, as she saw her little brother kick off his shoes, quickly roll off his socks, and start out towards the boat which a strong puff of wind had now blown quite close to the island shore.

"I'll be careful," he answered. "Mother said I could wade up as far as the wig-wag cut on my leg, and I'm not there yet."

Freddie had several scars and scratches on his legs, reminders of accidents he had suffered at different times. One scar was from a cut which he had got when he had fallen over the lawn mower about a year before. It was the biggest cut of all, and was near his right knee. He called it his "wig-wag" cut, because it was a sort of wavy scar, and when he wanted to go in wading his mother always told him never to go in water that would come above that cut, else he would get his trousers wet.

So now he was careful not to go out too far. He watched the water rising slowly up on his bare legs as he waded along on the sandy bottom of the lake towards the drifting boat.

"If you took a stick you could reach it now," called Flossie.

"I guess I could," Freddie said.

"I'll hand you a stick," Flossie offered, looking for one along the shore. There were many dead branches, blown from the trees, and she soon handed Freddie a long one. With it the little boy was able to pull the boat towards him slowly, and he had soon pushed the "nose", as he sometimes called the bow, against the shore of the island.

"Now I can get in!" laughed Flossie. "And I won't have to take off my shoes and socks either," and into the boat she scrambled.

"Oh!" exclaimed Freddie. "Are you going to get in the boat?"

"I am in," answered his sister. "Aren't you coming in, too?"

Freddie looked at the boat, at his sister, at the lake, and at his shoes and socks on the shore. Then he said:

"Well, it doesn't belong to us,"

"I know," said Flossie. "But you pulled it to shore and we can keep it till somebody comes for it. And we can make-believe have a ride in it. Mummy won't care as long as it's tied to the shore. Come on, Freddie!"

It seemed all right to Freddie when Flossie said this, especially as the boat was close against the shore. He put on his shoes and socks, drying his feet in the grass, and then he took his seat in the boat beside his little sister.

"Now we'll play going on a long voyage," she said. "We'll take a trip to New York and maybe we'll be shipwrecked."

"Like Tommy Todd's father," added Freddie.

"Yes. Just like him," said Flossie, "only make-believe, of course."

"And I'll be captain of the ship, and you can be a sailor," went on Freddie. "It'll be lots of fun!"

Bert and Nan had gone riding in the goat-cart to the other end of the island, Mr. Bobbsey was at his office and Mrs. Bobbsey, with Dinah, was working about Twin Camp, so there was no one to watch Flossie and Freddie. Mrs. Bobbsey supposed they were playing safely at the lake shore, and, as a matter of fact, they were on shore, though in the boat.

"I wonder whose it is?" said Freddie, when they had made a make-believe voyage safely to New York, after having been shipwrecked at Philadelphia—a place the little twins remembered, as one of their aunts lived in that city.

"Maybe it's a gypsy boat," said Freddie.

"Or else it's the one the blueberry boy had," added his sister.

"Oh, yes, maybe it is his!" cried Freddie. "And if it is, I suppose we ought to take it to him."

"How?" asked Flossie.

"Why, we can push it along the shore with sticks, 'cause there's no oars in it, and when we see him picking blueberries we can shout to him to come an' get his boat."

Flossie thought this over a few seconds. Then she said:

"Let's!"

In a little while the two twins were moving the

drifted boat along the shore by pushing the ends of their sticks into the soft bank. The boat was of good size, and it was flat-bottomed, which meant it would not easily tip over. Flossie and Freddie each knew how to row, though they had to have oars made especially for them. But they knew how to keep in the middle of a boat, and never thought of rocking it or changing seats, so they were much safer than most children of their age would have been.

Having lived near Lake Metoka all their lives, they knew more about boats and water than perhaps some small boys and girls do; and they could both swim, though, of course, not very far, nor were they allowed to try it in deep water.

"Oh, this is lots of fun!" cried Flossie, as she and Freddie poled the boat along.

"But we mustn't go too far," said Freddie, not quite sure whether or not his mother would think what he and his sister were doing was just right. "As soon as we see the blueberry boy we must give him his boat and go back home."

"If he wants to row us back, can't we let him?" asked Flossie.

"Yes, but he can't row, 'cause there are no oars in the boat," said Freddie.

"Maybe he has 'em with him. I guess that's what happened," went on the little girl. "You know we take the oars out of our boat and put them up on shore. And then maybe the blueberry boy forgot to tie his boat."

"And it blew away and we found it," finished

Freddie. "Come on, push hard, Flossie. Let's go fast and make believe we're a steamboat."

That suited Flossie, and they were soon pushing the boat along the shore quite fast. They went out past a little point on the island, some distance away from their own camp, the white tents of which they could see.

"Oh, how nice the wind is blowing!" cried Flossie, after a bit. "I don't hardly have to push at all, Freddie."

"That's good," he said. "We'll be a sailboat instead of a steamboat. If we only had a sail!"

"Maybe you could hold up your coat," suggested his sister. "Don't you remember that shipwreck story Mother read us? The men in the boat held up a blanket for a sail. We haven't any blanket, but if you held one end of your coat and I held the other it would be a sail."

"We'll do it!" cried Freddie, as he slipped off his jacket. It was small, but when he and his sister held it crosswise of the boat, the wind, which had begun to blow harder, sent the boat along faster than the children had been pushing it.

"Oh, this is fine!" Freddie cried. "I'm glad we played this game, Flossie."

"So'm I. But look how far out we are, Freddie!" Flossie suddenly cried. "We can't reach shore with our sticks."

Freddie looked and saw that this was so.

"I wonder if we can touch bottom out here," he said. "I'm going to try."

He let go of his coat, and as it happened that

Flossie did the same thing, the little jacket was blown into the water.

"Oh!" cried Flossie. "Oh! Oh!"

"I can get it!" excitedly shouted Freddie. "I'll reach it with my pushing stick."

He managed to do this, taking care not to lean too far over the edge so the boat would not tip. Then he caught the coat on the end of the stick and pulled his jacket into the boat.

"Oh, it's all wet!" cried Flossie.

Freddie did not stop to tell her that every time anything fell into the water it got wet. Instead, he began to search in his pockets.

"What's the matter—did you lose something?" asked Flossie.

"I guess we can eat 'em after they dry out," said Freddie, after a bit, pulling out some soaked sugar biscuits.

Freddie spread them out on one of the boat-seats where the sun would dry them, and then he wrung from his coat as much water as he could. Next he spread the jacket out to dry, Flossie helping him.

All this time the children failed to notice where they were going, but when they had seen that the soaked biscuits were getting dry and had eaten them, Freddie looked about and, pointing to shore, cried:

"Oh, look, Flossie!"

"We're going right towards a big, dark hole!" said the little girl.

"That isn't a hole—it's a cave," Freddie said.

"Maybe it's a pirate cave, and there'll be gold and jewels in it. The wind is blowing us and our boat right into it!"

And that was what was happening. The wind had changed, and, instead of blowing the boat away from the island, was blowing it towards it. And directly in front of Flossie and Freddie was a big hole in the steep bank of the island shore!

CHAPTER XIV

HELEN'S VISIT

WHILE the two children sat in the drifting row-boat, which was being slowly blown towards the island shore again, Flossie suddenly gave a little jump, which made the boat shake.

"What's the matter?" asked Freddie. "Did something bite you?" for his sister had started, just as you might do if a fly or a mosquito suddenly nipped your leg.

"No, nothing bit me," she answered. "But I felt a splash of rain on my nose and—— Oh, Freddie! Look! It's going to be a thunder-lightning storm!"

Freddie, whose eyes had seen nothing but the cave, now looked up at the sky. The blue had become covered with dark clouds, and in the west a dull rumble could be heard.

"I—I guess it is going to rain," said Freddie slowly.

"I know it is!" Flossie answered. "There's 'nother drop!"

"I felt one, too," said her brother. "It went right in my eye!" And he winked and blinked.

"And there's another one on my nose!" cried Flossie. "Oh, Freddie! What are we going to do? I haven't an umbrella!"

For a moment the little boy did not know what to do. He looked at his coat, but that was still wet, though it had been spread out on the seat to dry. He could not wrap that around Flossie, as he thought at first he might.

The wind, too, was blowing harder now, and there were little waves splashing against the side of the boat. But the wind did one good thing for the children—it blew the boat towards the shore so much faster, and the shore was where they wanted to be just now. They knew they had drifted out too far, and they were beginning to be afraid. The shore of the island looked very safe.

"We can get under a tree—that will be an umbrella for us," said Flossie. "Aren't you glad we're going on shore, Freddie?"

"Yes, but I guess we can get in a better place out of the rain than under a tree, Flossie."

"Then we'd better get," she said. "'cause it's raining hard now. I've got about ten splashes on my nose."

The big drops were beginning to fall faster. The clouds had quickly spread over the sky, which was now very dark, and the wind kept on blowing.

"Where can we go out of the storm?" asked the little girl.

"In there," answered her brother, pointing.

"What! In that dark hole?"

"It isn't a hole—it's a cave. An' maybe we'll find gold and diamonds in there, like in the book Mummy read to us. Come on. We can go into the cave, and we won't get wet at all. I'll take care of you."

"I—I'm not afraid," said Flossie slowly. "But I wish Snap was with us; or Whisker. I guess Whisker would like a cave."

"So would Snap," said Freddie. "But we can't get 'em now, so we've got to go in ourselves. Come on. And look out, 'cause the boat's going to bump."

And bump the boat did, a second later, against the shore of the island, close to the open mouth of the black cave. It was raining hard now, and Freddie helped Flossie out of the boat, and then, holding each other by the hand, the children ran towards the cavern. No matter what was in it, there they would be sheltered from the rain, they thought.

The cave, as Freddie and Flossie saw, could be entered from either the land or the water. At one side it was so low that a boat could be rowed into it for a little way. On the other one could walk into it by a little path that led through the trees. The water of the lake splashed into the cave a short distance, and then came to an end, making a sort of little bay, or cove, large enough for two or three boats. And the cave, as the children could see when their eyes became used to the darkness, was quite a large one.

"I wonder if anybody lives here," whispered Flossie, as she kept close to her brother.

"We live here now," he said. "Anyhow, we're going to stay here till the rain stops."

"Maybe a bear lives here," said Flossie.

"Pooh!" laughed Freddie. "There are no bears on Blueberry Island, or Daddy would have brought a gun. And he said I didn't even need my popgun, 'cause there wasn't a thing here to shoot. But I did bring my popgun."

"You haven't got it here now, though," said Flossie.

"I know I haven't. I felt it in the tent by the go-around beetles. I mean before the go-around beetles got away. But my popgun is there. I saw it. Only I haven't it now, so I can't shoot anything. But there's nothing to shoot, anyhow." Freddie added the last for fear his sister might be frightened in the dark cave.

It was very dark, especially back at the end, where Flossie and Freddie could see nothing. But by looking towards the place where they had come in, they could see daylight and the lake, which was now quite rough on account of the wind. They could also see the rain falling and splashing.

"I'm glad we're in here," said Flossie. "It's better than an umbrella."

"Lots better," agreed Freddie. "If we had some biscuits to eat we could stay here a long time, and live here."

"We couldn't sleep, 'cause we haven't any beds," declared Flossie.

"We could make beds of dried grass the way Bert told us to do if we went camping."

"But have you any more biscuits?" asked Flossie, going back to what her brother had first spoken of. "I'm hungry!"

"Only some crumbs," Freddie said, as he put his hands in the pockets of his coat, "and they're all soft and wet. We can't eat 'em."

"Well, we can go home when it stops raining," said Flossie, "an' Dinah'll give us lots to eat."

The two children were not frightened now. They stood in the cave, and looked out at the storm. It was raining harder than ever, and the thunder seemed to shake the big hole in the ground, while the lightning flashes lighted up the cave so Freddie and Flossie could look farther back into it.

But they could not see much, and if there was anyone or anything in the cave besides themselves, they did not know it. They saw the boat blown inside the cave, and it came to rest in the little cove, which was a sort of harbour.

Then, almost as quickly as it had started, the storm stopped. The wind ceased blowing, the rain no longer fell, the thunder rumbled no more and the lightning died out. For a few minutes longer Flossie and Freddie stayed in the cave, and then, as they were about to go out, the little girl grasped her brother by the arm and cried:

"Listen! Did you hear that?"

"What?" asked Freddie.

"A noise, like something growling!"

Freddie looked back over his shoulder into the dark part of the cave. Then, speaking as boldly as possible, he answered:

"I didn't hear it. Anyhow, I guess it was the wind. Come on, we'll go home!"

"Are we going back in the boat?" Flossie asked.

"I guess not," Freddie replied. "It'll be rough out on the lake—it always is after a storm. We can walk down the path to our camp. Besides, this isn't our boat. Maybe it belongs here and we'd better leave it."

"Then you'd better tie it," said Flossie. She and her brother had been told something of the care of boats, and one rule their father had given them was always to tie a boat when they got out of it. In the excitement of the storm the children had forgotten this at first, but now Flossie remembered it.

"Yes, I'll tie the boat," Freddie said, "and then whoever owns it can come and get it."

It did not take him long to scramble around to the edge of the little cove. Once there, he tied the rope of the boat fast to a large stone that was half buried in the ground. Making sure it would not slip off, Freddie came back to where Flossie waited for him.

She was quite ready to leave the cave, and soon the two children were outside under the trees that still were dripping with rain.

"Which way is home—I mean where our camp is?" asked Flossie, as she and Freddie walked along together.

"Down this way," he said. "See the path?"

Certainly there was a path leading away from the cave, but Freddie did not stop to think it might lead somewhere else than to Twin Camp. It was a nice, smooth path, though, and he and Flossie set out along it not at all worried.

"I'm hungry," said the little girl, "and I want to get home as soon as I can."

"I'm hungry, too," Freddie said. "We'll soon be home."

But the children might not have reached the camp soon, except that a little later they heard their names called in the wood, and, answering, they found Nan and Bert looking for them in the goat-cart, drawn by Whisker.

"Where in the world have you been?" asked Bert of his little brother and sister.

"Oh," answered Freddie, "we've been out in a boat and in a cave and we only had biscuits to eat and they were wet and——"

"We heard a noise in the cave. Maybe it's a bear, an' if it is Freddie can take his popgun the next time we go there. Can't you, Freddie?"

"Dear me!" laughed Nan. "What's it all about?"

Then the two small twins told more slowly what had happened to them, and Nan and Bert told their small brother and sister that, coming back from their little trip, they had found Mrs. Bobbsey much worried because she could not find Flossie and Freddie.

"Then it began to rain," said Nan, "and we were all as worried as could be. We looked at our boats, and when we found they were tied at the dock we didn't think you were out on the water. Then when it stopped raining Bert and I started out to find you and so did Sam, though he went a different way."

"And we called and called to you," said Bert. "Didn't you hear us shouting?"

"Maybe that was the noise we heard in the cave," said Freddie to his sister.

"What about this cave?" asked Bert. "Tell us where it is."

Then, riding back to camp in the goat-cart, the two small twins told again of the big hole in which they had taken refuge from the storm.

"I'd like to see that," Bert said. "We'll go there tomorrow."

"We can walk there, or Whisker can take us," said Freddie. "And then we can come home in the boat, but you'll have to take some oars, Bert."

"That's so—there *is* a boat!" exclaimed the elder Bobbsey boy. "I wonder whose it can be?"

But they did not find out at once, for the next day, when they all went to the cave—including Mr. and Mrs. Bobbsey—the boat was not there.

"Somebody untied it and took it away," said Freddie, as he pointed out the rock to which he had made fast the rope.

"Are you sure you tied it tightly?" asked his father.

"Yes. I made the same kind of knot you showed me," and Freddie told how he had done it. Flossie, too, was sure her brother had fastened the boat properly.

"Well, then somebody's been here in the cave," said Bert. "Say, it's a big place, Dad! Can't we get a lantern and see where it goes back there?" and he motioned to the dark part.

"Some time, maybe, but not now," said Mr. Bobbsey, who, with Mrs. Bobbsey, had walked along the island path to the cave while the children rode in the goat-cart. "I didn't know there was a cave on Blueberry Island. I don't believe many persons know it is here. But the boat might belong to some of the berry pickers, and they hunted for it until they found it."

"Did the blueberry pickers make the funny noise in the cave?" asked Flossie.

"I don't know," replied her father. "I don't hear any noise now. I presume it was only the wind."

Mr. Bobbsey and Bert, lighting matches, went a short way back into the cave, but they could see very little, and the children's father said they would look again some other day.

"But, Flossie and Freddie, you mustn't come here alone again," said Mr. Bobbsey.

"If it rains and we're near here can't we come in if we haven't an umbrella?" asked Freddie.

"Well, yes, perhaps if it rains. But you mustn't go out in a drifting boat again, rain or no rain," ordered Mr. Bobbsey.

Flossie and Freddie promised they would not, as they always did, and then the camping family started back for their tents.

"What do you think of that cave, the boat's being taken and all that's happened?" asked Mrs. Bobbsey in a whisper to her husband, as they walked towards camp together.

"I don't know what to think," he said slowly.

"Do you suppose the gypsies could be in there?"

"Well, they might. But don't let the children know. They are having a good time here and there's no need, as yet, to frighten them."

For the next few days there were happy times in Twin Camp. The children went on many rides in the goat-cart and had other fun. Then, one afternoon when they were all sitting near the tents waiting for Dinah to get dinner, they saw a steamer heading towards the little dock.

"Oh, maybe it's company!" cried Flossie, clapping her hands.

And so it proved, for when the boat landed Mrs. Porter and her little girl, Helen, got off.

"We came to see how you were," said Mrs. Porter. "Helen wanted a trip on the water, so we came on the excursion boat. We're going back this evening. How are you?"

"Very well, indeed," said Mrs. Bobbsey, "and glad to see you. Helen can play with Flossie and Freddie."

"Did you see any of the gypsies, and did they have my talking doll?" asked Helen as soon as she had taken off her hat in the tent and had gone outside to play with the two small Bobbsey twins.

CHAPTER XV

THE DOLL'S DRESS

"HAVEN'T you got your lost doll back yet?" asked Freddie, as he moved over on a board, nailed between two trees, to make room for Helen to sit down between him and Flossie.

"No. I haven't found Mollie," answered the little girl, who had come to visit her friends. "I guess she's a gypsy by this time."

"Helen, are you sure a gypsy man took your doll?" asked Nan, who had been sent out by her mother to see if the little ones were all right.

"Yes, I'm sure," answered Helen. "I left her in the garden; and, besides, didn't Johnnie Marsh and me both see the gypsy man running off with her?"

"Well, maybe it did happen that way," said Nan. "But what makes you think we might have seen that gypsy man here, Helen?"

"'Cause Johnnie Marsh said gypsies were camped on Blueberry Island."

"We haven't seen any yet," remarked Bert, who had come out to ask the little girl visitor about some of his boy friends in Lakeport.

"Maybe they're hiding 'cause they've got Helen's

doll," said Flossie. "And maybe they're in the cave Freddie and I found."

"Did you find a cave?" asked Helen. "My mamma read me a story once about a cave and a giant that lived in it. Did your cave have a giant inside?"

"It had a noise!" answered Flossie excitedly. "Freddie heard it! But we didn't go to see what it was. Are you hungry, Helen?" she asked, suddenly changing the subject.

"Yes, I am. I only had some cake and ice cream on the boat."

"We're going to have ice cream!" Freddie cried. "I wish dinner would hurry up and be ready."

It was not long after this that Dinah rang the gong which told that the meal was cooked, and soon they were all seated in the dining-tent making merry over it. Mrs. Porter told how Helen had been asking, ever since the Bobbseys had come to Blueberry Island, to be brought for a visit.

"She says that maybe the gypsies who took her doll are here," went on Mrs. Porter, "though I tell her she will never see Mollie again. But Helen begged hard to come, and so—here we are."

"And we're very glad to see you," said Mrs. Bobbsey. "Can't you stay longer than just until this evening?"

"No, not this time, as we didn't bring any extra clothes with us. But Helen might come later for a visit of a few days."

"Oh, yes, please let her come!" begged Flossie.

"We'll see," said Mrs. Porter. "Did you find Snap?" she asked Bert.

"No, we haven't heard anything of him. I was going to ask if you had," and he looked anxiously at Helen's mother.

"No, I haven't heard a word about your pet," answered Mrs. Porter, "though I've asked all your boy friends, and so has Helen. Tommy Todd and the others say they are keeping watch for Snap, and if they see him they'll let you know. Has anything else happened since you've been here?" she asked Mr. and Mrs. Bobbsey.

"Nothing much," answered Nan's mother. "We have had a lovely time camping, and——"

"Flossie's and my go-around beetles broke out of their box!" cried Freddie, and then he begged his mother's pardon for interrupting her when she was speaking. His mother smiled, excused him, and then she let him and Flossie, in turn, tell about the missing toys.

"Come on, we'll play hide-and-seek," proposed Flossie after dinner, while her father and mother and Mrs. Porter were still sitting about the table talking. "Do you and Nan want to play, Bert?" she asked her elder brother.

"No, Flossie," he answered with a smile. "I'm going to help Sam cut wood for the campfire. We're going to have a marshmallow roast tonight."

"Oh, I just wish I could stay!" cried Helen. "I love to roast marshmallows!"

"We'll roast some when you come again," said

Nan, who was going to do some sewing, so she could not play with the smaller children just then. Soon the game of hide-and-seek began.

Freddie said he would hide first, and let both girls hunt for him. He thought he could hide so well that he could fool them both, and still get "home safe" before they spied him.

So while Flossie and Helen "blinded" by hiding their faces in their arms against a tree, Freddie stole quietly off to hide. He found a good place behind a pile of brushwood, and there he cuddled up in a little heap and waited until he heard the two girls searching for him.

By peeping through the brush Freddie could see Helen and his sister looking all about for him —behind trees, down back of fallen logs, and in clumps of ferns.

Then Freddie saw the girls go far enough away from "home", which was a big oak tree, so that he thought he would have a chance to run in "free".

This he did, and how surprised Flossie and Helen were when they saw him dash out from the pile of brushwood!

"I'll let you hide," said Freddie, though if the game was played by the rules it would be his turn to hide again, as he had not been caught.

So this time the little boy hid his head in his arms and began counting up to a hundred by fives, and when he had called out loudly: "Ninety-five —one hundred! Ready or not, I'm coming!" he opened his eyes and began searching.

Freddie had to be more careful about going away from the "home" tree than had the two little girls. Either one of them could have spied him and have run to touch "home" before he did. But Freddie was all alone hunting for his sister and Helen, and when he had his back turned one or the other might run in ahead of him.

"But I'll find 'em," he told himself. "I'll spy 'em both and then it will be my turn to hide."

Meanwhile, Flossie and Helen were well hidden. Flossie had found two logs lying on a pile of leaves, not far from the "home" tree, and she had crawled down in between them, pulling leaves over her. Only her nose stuck out, so she could breathe, and no one could have seen her until they were very close.

Helen had picked out a hollow stump in which to hide. It was deep enough for her to get inside, and the bottom was covered with old leaves, so it was soft and not very dirty. Helen had been given an old dress of Flossie's to put on to play in, so she would not soil her own white one.

"I'm going to have a good place to hide," thought Helen, as she climbed up on a pile of stones outside the old stump and jumped down inside, crouching there.

Then she waited for Freddie to come to find her, and as there was a crack in the stump, she could look out and see where he was. As soon as he got far enough away from "home", Flossie, who was nearer the oak tree, would run in free—and then she would try to reach it.

Meanwhile she crouched in the hollow stump, trying not to laugh or cough or sneeze, for if she did that Freddie would hear and know where she was. Helen saw something white in the stump with her. At first she thought it was a piece of paper, but when she picked it up she knew it was cloth. And as she looked at it her eyes grew big with wonder.

Without stopping to think that she was playing the hide-and-seek game, Helen suddenly stood up in the hollow stump, her head showing above the edge like a Jack-in-the-box. In her hand she held the white thing she had found.

Flossie, from her hiding place between the two logs, could look over and see what Helen was doing. Seeing her standing up in plain sight, Flossie, in a loud whisper, called to her friend:

"Get down! Get down! Freddie will see you and then you'll be it! Get down!"

"But look! Look at what I found! In the hollow stump!" answered Helen. "Oh, I must show you!"

"No! Get down!" cried Flossie, pulling more leaves over herself. "Here comes Freddie. He'll see you!"

The little boy was coming from the "home" tree. He caught sight of Helen, and cried:

"There's Helen! There's Helen! I see her in the hollow stump!"

"I don't care if I am it," Helen answered. "Look what I found!"

"What is it?" asked Flossie, sitting up amid the leaves.

"It's the dress Mollie wore when the gypsy took her away!" exclaimed Helen. "Oh, my doll must be somewhere on this island!" And holding the white object high above her head, she ran towards Flossie.

CHAPTER XVI

SNOOP IS MISSING

THE children suddenly lost interest in the game of hide-and-seek. Freddie thought no more of spying Flossie or Helen. Flossie no longer cared about hiding down between the two logs, and Helen did not care about anything but the white dress she was holding up as she scrambled out of the hollow stump.

"It's my doll's dress!" she said over and over again. "It's my lost doll's dress!"

"Are you sure?" asked Flossie, as she shook the leaves from her dress and hair, and came over to her friend.

"Course I'm sure!" answered Helen. "Look, here's a place where I mended the dress after Mollie tore it when she was playing with Grace Lavine's dolly one day."

Mollie hadn't really torn her dress. Helen had done it herself lifting her out of the doll carriage, but she liked to pretend the doll had done it.

"Let's see the torn place," said Flossie, and Helen showed where a hole had been sewed.

"I 'member it," Helen went on, " 'cause I sewed it crooked. I can sew better now. It's my doll's dress, all right."

"It's all wet," said Freddie. "Maybe the gypsies live around here," he went on, "and they washed your doll's dress and hung it on the stump to dry."

"Maybe!" agreed Helen, who was ready to believe anything, now that she had found something belonging to her doll.

"No gypsies live around here," said Flossie, " 'cause we haven't seen any. But maybe they live in the cave."

"The cave's far off," said Freddie. "But it's funny about that dress."

"I—I found it when I hid in the stump," explained the little visitor. "First I thought it was a piece of paper, but as soon as I touched it I knew it wasn't. Oh, now if I could only find Mollie!"

"Maybe she's in the stump, too," Freddie said. "If the gypsies washed her dress they'd have to cover her up with leaves or bark so she wouldn't get cold while her dress was drying."

"The gypsies didn't wash her dress," said Helen.

"How do you know?" asked Flossie.

" 'Cause nobody washes dresses an' makes 'em all up in a heap an' puts 'em in a hollow stump," Helen went on. "You've got to hang a dress straight on a line to make it dry."

"That's so," said Flossie. "You only roll a dress up the way this one was rolled when you sprinkle it to iron, don't you, Helen?"

"Yes. Oh, I do wish I could find my Mollie!"

"Well, she must be somewhere around here if she isn't in the stump," insisted Freddie. "If the gypsies took off her dress they must have dropped the doll. Let's look!"

This was what the two little girls wanted to do, so with Freddie to help they began poking about with sticks in the leaves that were piled around the stump. They searched for some time, but could find no trace of the lost doll.

"We'd better go and tell my mother and yours, too," said Flossie. "Maybe they'll get a policeman and he'll find the gypsies and your dolly, Helen."

"All right—come on!"

Out of breath, the children ran to the tents where Mrs. Potter was just thinking about going in search of her little girl, as it was nearly time for the steamboat to come back for them.

"Oh, I found Mollie's dress! I found Mollie's dress!" cried Helen, waving it over her head.

"It was in a stump!" added Freddie.

"And it was all wet from being rained on, I guess," said Flossie, for indeed the doll's dress was still damp, and very likely it had been out in the rain. That stump would hold water for some time, like a big, wooden pitcher.

Mrs. Porter was very much surprised to hear the news, and thought perhaps her little girl was mistaken. But when she had looked carefully at the dress, she knew it was one she herself had made for Helen when that little girl was a baby.

"But how did it come on this island?" she asked.

"It must have been dropped by the gypsies," said Mr. Bobbsey. "In spite of what they said to us some one of them must have picked up the doll

and carried her away for some little gypsy girl.
And the gypsies must have been on this island.
Some of the blueberry pickers said they saw them,
but when I looked I could not find them. By that
time they must have gone away."

"And did they take my doll with them?" asked
Helen.

"Well, I'm afraid they did," said Mr. Bobbsey.
"If they wanted your doll badly enough to take her
away so boldly, as they did from the garden, they'd
probably keep her, once they had her safe. It isn't
every day they can get a talking doll, you know."

"I wish there was some way of getting Helen's
doll back," said Mrs. Porter. "She does nothing but
wish for her every day. She has other dolls——"

"But I liked Mollie best," Helen said. "I want
her. If she only knew I had her dress she might
come to me," she added wistfully.

"She might, if she were a fairy doll," said Mrs.
Bobbsey, as she patted Helen on the head. "But
we'll look as carefully as we can for your little girl's
doll, Mrs. Porter. If Mollie is on this island we'll
find her."

"And I'll leave this dress here," said Helen, "so
you can put it on her when you do find her. Then
she won't take cold."

"I'll wash the dress and have Dinah iron it for
you," promised Flossie. "I can't iron very well."

"Thank you," said Helen. "Oh, I'm so glad I
came here, for I found part of Mollie, anyhow."

Helen and her mother left Blueberry Island,
promising to come again some day, and Flossie and

Freddie said they would, in the meanwhile, look as well as they could for the lost doll.

That night, in front of the tents, there was a marshmallow roast. The Bobbsey children, with long sticks, toasted the soft candies over the blaze, until the marshmallows puffed out like balloons and were coloured a pretty brown. Then they ate them.

Flossie and Freddie dropped about as many marshmallows in the fire as they toasted, but Bert and Nan at last showed the small twins how to do it, and then Freddie toasted a marshmallow for his father and Flossie made one nice and brown for her mother.

"I dropped mine in the dirt, after I cooked it," said Freddie to his father, as he came running up with the hot marshmallow, "but I guess you can eat it."

"I'll try," laughed Mr. Bobbsey, and he brushed off all the dirt he could, but had to chew the rest, for Freddie stood right in front of his father, to make sure the marshmallow was eaten.

"Is it good?" asked the little boy.

"Fine!" cried Mr. Bobbsey. "But I can't eat any more," he said quickly, "because I might get indigestion."

"Then I'll eat 'em," said Freddie. "I'm not afraid of id—idis—idisgestion."

It was jolly fun toasting marshmallows at the camp-fire, but as everything must come to an end some time, this did also, and the children went to bed and the camp was quiet, except that now and then Whisker gave a gentle "Baa-a-a-a!" from his resting place under a tree, and Snoop, the black cat, purred in his sleep.

The next day it rained, so the twins could not go to look for the doll as they wanted to. They had to stay around the tents, though when the shower slackened they were allowed to go out with their raincoats and boots on.

Towards night the sun came out, and they all went down to the dock to meet the steamboat, for Mr. Bobbsey had gone over to the mainland after dinner, to attend to some business at the lumber office, and was coming back on the last boat.

It was after supper that Dinah, coming into the dining-tent to clear away the dishes, caused some excitement when she asked:

"Have any of you-all seen Snoop?"

"What? Is our cat gone?" asked Bert.

"Well, I haven't seen him since Flossie an' Freddie were playing hitch him up like a horse to a cigar-box wagon," went on Dinah. "He came out to me an' I gave him some milk, an' now, when I called him to come an' get his supper, he isn't here!"

Flossie and Freddie looked at each other. So did Nan and Bert. Even Mr. Bobbsey seemed surprised. But he said:

"Oh, I guess he just went off in the woods for a rest after Flossie and Freddie mauled him when they were playing with him. Go call him, Bert."

So Bert went out in front of the tent and called: "Snoop! Snoop! Hi, Snoop, where are you?"

But no Snoop came. Then Flossie and Freddie called, and so did Nan, while Sam went farther into the woods among the trees. But the big black cat, that the children loved so dearly, was missing. Snoop did not come to his supper that night.

CHAPTER XVII

FREDDIE IS CAUGHT

"LISTEN, everybody!"

"Wasn't that Snoop?"

Bert and Nan suddenly made these exclamations as they, with the rest of the Bobbsey family, were sitting in the main tent after supper. The lanterns had been lighted, the mosquito net drawn over the flap of the tent, to keep out the insects, and the camping family was spending a quiet hour before going to bed.

Bert thought he heard, in the woods outside, a noise that sounded like the missing cat Snoop, and Nan, also, thought she heard the same sound.

They all listened, Mr. Bobbsey looking up from his book, while Flossie and Freddie ceased their play. Mrs. Bobbsey stopped her sewing.

"There it is again!" exclaimed Nan, as from the darkness outside the tent there came a strange sound.

"What is it?" asked Mrs. Bobbsey. "It doesn't sound like Snoop."

"Maybe it's Snap!" exclaimed Freddie. "He used to howl like that."

"It did sound a bit like a dog's howl," admitted Bert. "May I go out and see what it is, Dad?"

"I'll take a look," said Mr. Bobbsey. He stepped to the flap of the tent and listened. The sound came again, and he went outside, while Bert went near the tent opening to listen. He, as well as his father, then heard another noise—that made by someone walking across the ground, stepping on and breaking small sticks.

"Who's there?" suddenly called Mr. Bobbsey, exactly, as Bert said afterwards, like a soldier sentinel on guard. "Who's there?"

"It's me—Sam," was the answer. "I heard some queer noise, Mr. Bobbsey, an' Dinah said as how I'd better get up and see what it was."

"Oh, all right, Sam. We heard it, too. Listen again."

Sam stood still, and Mr. Bobbsey remained quietly outside the big tent. Sam and Dinah lived in a smaller tent not far away, and they usually went to bed early, so Sam had had to get up when the queer noise sounded.

Suddenly it came again, and this time Bert, who had stuck his head out between the flaps of the tent, called:

"There it is!"

"Who! Who! Who!" came the sound, and as Mr. Bobbsey heard it he gave a laugh.

"Nothing but an owl," he said. "I should have known it at first, only I couldn't hear well in the tent. You may go back to bed, Sam, it's only an owl."

"Only an owl, Mr. Bobbsey! Yes, I reckon as how it is; but I don't like t' hear it just the same."

"You don't? Why not, Sam?"

"'Cause they generally bring bad luck. I don't like the sound of that owl's singin' no how!"

"He wasn't singing, Sam!" laughed Bert, after he had called to the rest of the family inside the tent and told them the cause of the noise.

"Ha! Is that you, Bert?" asked the handyman. "Well, maybe an owl doesn't sing like a canary bird, but they make a mournful sound, an' I don't like it. It means bad luck, that's what it means! An' you-all'd better get to bed!"

"Oh, I'm not afraid, Sam. We thought it was Snoop mewing, or Snap howling, maybe. You didn't see anything of our lost dog, did you?"

"Not a smitch. An' I sure would like t' have him back."

"Ask him if he or Dinah saw Snoop," called Flossie.

Bert asked the handyman this, but Sam had seen nothing of the pet either.

"Oh dear!" sighed Freddie. "Both our pets gone—Snap and Snoop! I wish they'd come back."

"Maybe they will," said his mother kindly. "It's time for you to go to bed now, and maybe the morning will bring good news. Snap or Snoop may be back by that time."

"That's what we've been thinking about poor Snap for a long while," grumbled Nan.

"Well, I'm afraid Snap *is* lost for good," said Mrs. Bobbsey. "He never stayed away so long before. But Snoop may be back in the morning.

He may have just wandered off. It isn't the first time he has been away all night."

"Only once or twice," said Bert, who came back to the book he was reading. "And both times it was because he got shut by accident in places where he couldn't get out."

"Maybe that's what's happened this time," suggested Nan. "We ought to look around the island."

"We will—tomorrow," declared Bert.

"And look in the cave Flossie and I found," urged Freddie. "Maybe Snoop is there."

"We'll look," promised his brother.

When Flossie and Freddie were taken to their cots by their mother, Flossie, when she had finished her regular prayers, added:

"An' please don't let 'em take Whisker."

"What do you mean by that, Flossie?" asked her mother.

"I mean I was prayin' that they shouldn't take our goat," said the little girl.

"I want to pray that, too!" cried Freddie, who had hopped into bed. "Why didn't you tell me you were going to pray that, Flossie?"

"'Cause it just popped into my head. But you stay in bed, an' I'll pray it for you," and she added: "Please, Freddie says the same thing!"

Then she covered herself up and almost before Mrs. Bobbsey had left both children were fast asleep.

"Poor little souls!" said their mother softly. "They do miss their pets so! I hope the cat and dog can be found, and Helen's doll, too. It's strange that so many things are missing. I wonder who Flossie meant by 'they'. I must ask her."

And the next morning the little girl, when reminded of her petition the night before and asked who she thought might take the goat, said:

"They is the gypsies, of course! They take everything! Blueberry Tom said so. And I didn't want them to get Whisker too."

"Who in the world is Blueberry Tom?" asked Mrs. Bobbsey.

"He's the boy who was so hungry," explained Freddie. "He came to the island to pick early blueberries only there wasn't any."

"Oh, now I remember," Mrs. Bobbsey said with a laugh. "Well, I don't believe there are any gypsies on this island to take anything. Snoop must have just wandered off."

"Then we'll find him!" exclaimed Nan.

During the next few days a search was made for the missing black cat. The twins, sometimes riding in their goat-cart, and again going on foot, went over a good part of the island, calling for Snoop. But he did not answer. Sam, too, wandered about getting firewood, and also calling for the lost pet. Mr. Bobbsey made inquiries of the boatman and the man who kept the lemonade stall, but none of them had seen Snoop.

Bert printed, with a lead pencil, paper signs, offering a reward for any news of Snoop, and these were tacked up on trees about the island so the blueberry pickers might see them. But though many read them, none had seen Snoop, and, of course, Snap was missing before the Bobbseys came to camp, so, naturally, he would not be on the island.

But in spite of the missing Snap and Snoop, the Bobbsey twins had lots of fun in camp. During the day they played all sorts of games, went on long walks with their father and mother, or for trips on the lake. Sometimes they even rowed to other islands not far from Blueberry Island.

The fishing was good, and Freddie and Bert often brought home a nice catch for dinner or supper. Whisker, the big white goat, was a jolly pet. He was as gentle as a dog and never seemed to get tired of pulling the twins in the little cart, though the roads of the island were not as smooth as those in Lakeport.

But though the twins had fun, they never gave up thinking that, some day, they would find Snap and Snoop again.

"And maybe Helen's doll, too," said Flossie. "We'll hunt for her some more."

"But it's easier to hunt for Snoop," said Freddie, " 'cause he can shout back when you call him."

"How can a cat shout?" asked his sister.

"Well, he can go 'miaou', can't he?" Freddie asked, "an' isn't that shouting?"

"I—I guess so," Flossie answered. "Oh, Freddie, I know what let's do!" she cried suddenly.

"What? Make mud pies again? I'm tired of 'em. 'Sides, Mummy just put clean things on us."

"No, not make mud pies—I'm tired of that, too. Let's go off by ourselves and hunt Snoop.

You know every time we've gone very far from camp we've had to go with Nan and Bert; and you know when you hunt cats you ought to be quiet, an' two can be more quiet than three or four."

"That's right," agreed Freddie, after thinking it over.

"Then let's just us two go," went on Flossie. "We won't get lost."

"No, course not," said Freddie. "I can go all over the island, and I won't let you be lost. Snoop knows us better than he does Nan and Bert anyhow, 'cause we play with him more."

"And if we find him," went on Flossie, "and he's too tired to walk home we'll carry him. I'll carry his head part an' you can carry his tail."

"No, I want to carry his head."

"I chose his head first!" said Flossie. "The tail is nicest anyhow."

"Then why don't you carry that?"

"'Cause it's so flopsy. It never stays still, and when it flops in my face it tickles me. Please you carry the tail end, Freddie."

"All right, Flossie, I will. But we had better go now, or maybe Mummy or Dinah might come out and tell us not to go. Come on!"

So, hand in hand, now and then looking back to make sure no one saw them to order them back, Flossie and Freddie started out to search for the lost Snoop. They wandered here and there about the island, at first not very far from the camp. When they were near the tents they did not call the cat's name very loudly for fear of being heard.

"We can call him loud enough when we get farther away," said Freddie.

"Yes," agreed his sister. "Anyhow he isn't near the tents or he'd have come back before this."

So the two little twins wandered farther and farther away until they were well to the middle of the island, and out of sight of the white tents.

"Snoop! Snoop! Snoop!" they called, but though they heard many noises made by the birds, the squirrels and insects of the woods, there was no answering cry from their cat.

After a while they came to a place where a little brook flowed between green, mossy banks. It was a hot day and the children were warm and tired.

"Oh, I'm going to paddle!" cried Freddie, sitting down and taking off his shoes and socks.

"You hadn't better," said Flossie. "Mummy mightn't like it."

"I'll tell her how nice it was when I get home," said the little fellow, "and then she'll say it was all right. Come on, Flossie."

"No, I've got clean white socks on and I don't want to get 'em all dirty."

"Huh! They've got some dirt on 'em now."

"Well, they aren't wet and they'd get wet if I went in paddling."

"Not if you took 'em off."

"Yes they would, 'cause I never can get my feet dry on the grass like you do. You go in, Freddie, and I'll sit here an' watch you."

So Freddie stepped into the cool water and shouted with glee. Then he waded out a little farther and soon a queer look came over his face. Flossie saw her brother sink down until the brook came up to his knees, while Freddie cried:

"Oh, I'm caught! I'm caught. Flossie, help me!"

CHAPTER XVIII

FLOSSIE IS TANGLED

FLOSSIE Bobbsey, who had been sitting on the cleanest and dryest log she could find near the edge of the stream to watch Freddie paddle, jumped up as she heard him cry. She had been wishing she was with him, white socks or none.

"Oh, Freddie, what's the matter?" she cried. "What's happened?"

"I—I'm caught!" he answered. "Can't you see I'm caught?"

"But how?" she questioned eagerly. "You aren't caught in a trap like Snap was, are you?"

"No, it isn't a trap—it's sticky mud," Freddie said. "My feet are stuck in the mud!"

"Oh—oh!" said Flossie, and a queer look came over her face. "You are stuck in the mud! How did you do it, Freddie?"

"I didn't do it! It did it! I just stepped in a soft place, and now when I pull one foot out the other sticks in deeper. Can't you help me out, Flossie?"

"Yes, I'll help you out!" she cried, and she ran down to the edge of the stream, as though she intended to wade out to where poor Freddie was trying to pull his feet loose from the sticky mud.

"Oh, don't come in! Don't come in!" cried

Freddie, waving her back with his hand. "You'll be stuck, too!"

Flossie stood still on the edge of the little brook. She looked at Freddie, who was in the middle of the stream, too far out for Flossie to reach with her outstretched hands, though she tried to do so.

"Can't you pull your feet out?" she asked.

"No!" answered Freddie. "I can't, for I've tried. As soon as I get one foot up a little way the other goes down in deeper."

"Then I'll go and call Mother!"

"No, don't do that!" begged Freddie. "Maybe if you would get a long stick, Flossie, and hold it out to me, I could sort of pull myself out."

"Oh, I know. It's like the picture in my story book of the boy who fell through the ice, and his sister held out a long pole to him and he pulled himself out. Wait a minute, Freddie, and I'll get the stick. I'm glad you didn't fall through the ice, though, 'cause you'd get cold maybe."

"This water is nice and warm," said Freddie. "But I don't like the mud I'm stuck in, 'cause it makes me feel so tickly between the toes."

"I'll help you out," said Flossie. "Wait a minute."

She searched about on the bank until she found a long smooth branch of a tree. Holding to one end of this, she held the other end out to her brother. Freddie had to turn half around to get hold of it as his back was towards Flossie, and she could not cross the brook.

"Now hold tight!" cried the little boy. "I'm going to pull!"

Flossie braced her feet in the sand on the bank of the brook and her brother began to pull himself out of the mud. His feet had sunk down to quite a depth, and when he first pulled he made Flossie slide along the ground until she cried:

"Oh, Freddie, you're going to make me stuck, too! Don't pull me into the water!"

Freddie stopped just in time, with the toes of Flossie's shoes almost in the water.

"Did you pull loose a little bit?" she asked.

"Yes, a little. But I don't want to pull you in, Flossie. If you could only hang on to a tree or a rock, then I wouldn't drag you along."

"Maybe I can hang on to this tree," and Flossie pointed to one near by. "If I can stretch my arms I can reach it."

"Look for a longer tree branch to hold out to me," said Freddie, and when his sister had found one she could reach one end to her brother, keep the other end in her right hand, and with her left arm hold on to a small tree. The tree braced Flossie against being pulled along the bank, and when next Freddie tried, he dragged his feet and legs safely from the sticky mud, and could wade out on the hard, gravelly bottom of the brook.

"I guess that was a mudhole where some fish used to live," said the little fellow, as he came ashore, a little bit frightened.

"Your feet are all muddy," said Flossie, "and you are all wet around your knees."

"Oh, that'll dry," said Freddie. "And I can wash the mud off my feet. It was awful sticky."

It certainly seemed to be, for it took quite a while to wash it off his bare feet and legs. Freddie stood for some time in the brook, where there was a white, pebbly bottom, and used bunches of moss for a bath sponge.

When Freddie had put on his socks and shoes, the two children set out again, wandering here and there, calling for the black cat. But either he did not hear them or he would not answer, and when, after an hour or two, they got back to camp, they had not found their pet.

"Where have you two been?" asked Mrs. Bobbsey. "I was just getting anxious about you."

"We've been looking for Snoop," said Flossie.

"And I went paddling an' got stuck in the mud, and my shorts got a little wet, and Flossie's shoes and socks got wet an' muddy, but we walked in tall grass and we're not very muddy now," said Freddie, all out of breath, but anxious to get the worst over with at once.

"Oh, you shouldn't have gone paddling!" cried Mrs. Bobbsey.

"You didn't tell me not to—not today you didn't tell me," Freddie defended himself.

"No, because I didn't think you'd do such a thing," replied his mother. "I can't tell you every day the different things you mustn't do—there are too many of them."

"But there are so many things we can do too— oh, just lots of them."

"Yes, and the things we may do and the things we're not to do are just awful hard to tell apart sometimes, Mummy," put in Flossie.

"Yes'm, they are," added Freddie. "And how are we to know every single time what we're to do and what we're not to do?"

"Suppose you try stopping before you do a thing to ask yourselves whether you ought to do it or not, and not wait until after the thing is done to ask yourselves that question," suggested Mrs. Bobbsey. "That might help."

"Well, I won't go paddling any more today," promised the little fellow. "But I didn't think I'd get stuck in the mud."

"And so you couldn't find Snoop," remarked Mr. Bobbsey at supper that night. "Well, it's too bad. I guess I'll have to get you another dog and cat."

"No, don't—just yet, please," said Nan. "Maybe we'll find our own, and we never could love any new ones as we love Snap and Snoop."

"No, we couldn't!" declared Flossie, while Freddie nodded his head in agreement with her.

"But you could get us some new go-around beetles," the little girl went on.

"That's so," remarked Mr. Bobbsey. "It's queer where they went to. Well, I'll see if I can get any more, though I may have to send to New York. But you two little ones must not go off by yourselves again, looking for Snoop."

"Could we go to look for Snap?" asked Freddie, as if that was different.

"No, not for Snap either. You must stay around camp unless someone goes along with you to the woods."

It was a few days after this, when Mrs. Bobbsey, with the four twins, went out to pick blueberries, that they met a number of women and children who also had baskets and pails. But none of them was filled with the fruit which, now, was at its best.

"What is the matter with the berries?" asked Mrs. Bobbsey. "We have been able to pick only a few. The bushes seem to have been cleaned of all the ripe ones."

"That's what they have," said Blueberry Tom, who was with the other pickers. "And it's the gypsies who are getting the berries, too."

"Are you sure?" asked Mrs. Bobbsey. "We haven't seen any gypsies on the island."

"They don't stay here all the while," said Tom. "They have their camp over on the main shore, and they row over here and get the berries when they're ripest. That's why there aren't any for us—the gypsies get 'em before we have a chance. They're picking blueberries as soon as it's light enough to see."

"Well, I suppose they have as much right to them as we have," said Mrs. Bobbsey. "But I would like to get enough for some pies."

"I can show you where there are more than there are around here," offered Tom. "It's a little far to walk, though."

"Well, we're not tired, for we just came out,"

said Mrs. Bobbsey. "So if you'll take us there, Tom, we'll be very thankful."

"Come on," said the boy, whose face was once more covered with blue stains. "I'll show you."

The other berry pickers, who did not believe Tom knew of a better place, said they would stay where they were, and, perhaps, by hard work they might fill their pails or baskets, and so Tom and the Bobbseys went off by themselves.

Tom, indeed, seemed to know where, on the island, was one spot where the largest and sweetest blueberries grew, and the gypsies, if the members of the tribe did come to gather the fruit, seemed to have passed by this place.

"Oh, what lots of them!" cried Bert, as he saw the laden bushes.

"Yes, there's more than I thought," said Tom. "I'll get my basket full here all right."

Soon all were picking, though Flossie and Freddie may have put into their mouths as many as went in their two baskets. But their mother did not expect them to gather much fruit.

They had picked enough for several pies, and Mrs. Bobbsey was looking about for the two smaller twins who had wandered off a little way, when she heard Flossie scream.

"What is it?" asked her mother quickly. "Is it a snake?" and she started to run towards her little girl.

"Maybe she's stuck in the mud, as Freddie was!" exclaimed Bert.

"Mother! Mother!" cried Flossie. "Come and get me!"

"She—she's all tangled up in a net!" cried the voice of Freddie. "Oh, come here!"

Mrs. Bobbsey, Nan, Bert and Tom ran towards the sound of the children's voices.

CHAPTER XIX

THE TWINS FALL DOWN

AGAIN Flossie cried:

"I'm all tangled! I'm all tangled up! Come and help me to get out!"

"What in the world can she mean?" asked Mrs. Bobbsey.

"I'm sure I don't know," answered Bert.

"What did Freddie say about a net?" asked Nan, as she stumbled and spilled her blueberries. She was going to stop to pick them up.

"Never mind them," her mother said. "Let them go. We must see what the matter is with Flossie."

They saw a few seconds later, as they came to a turn in the path. On top of a little hill, in a place where there was a grassy spot with bushes growing all around it, they saw Flossie and Freddie.

Freddie was dancing around very much excited, but Flossie was standing still, and they soon saw the reason why. She was entangled in a net that was spread out on the ground and partly raised up on the bushes. It was like a fish net which the children had often seen the men or boys use in Lake Metoka, but the meshes, or holes in it, were smaller, so that only a very little fish could have slipped through. And the cord from which the net was woven was not as heavy as that of the fish nets.

"Flossie's caught! Flossie's caught!" cried Freddie, still dancing about.

"Come and get me loose! Come and get me loose!" Flossie begged.

"Mother's coming!" answered Mrs. Bobbsey. "But how in the world did it happen?"

She did not wait for an answer. As soon as she came near, she started to rush right into the net herself to lift out her little girl. But Bert, seeing what would happen, cried:

"Look out, Mother! You'll get tangled up, too. See! the net is caught on Flossie's shoes and around her legs and arms. She must have fallen right into it."

"She did," said Freddie. "We were walking along, picking berries, and all of a sudden Flossie was tangled in the net. I tried to get her out, but I got tangled, too, only I took my knife and cut some of the cords."

"And that's what we've got to do," said Mrs. Bobbsey. "The net is so entangled around Flossie that we'll never get her out otherwise. Have you a knife, Bert?"

"Yes, Mother. Stand still, Flossie!" he called to his little sister. "The more you move the worse you get tangled."

With his mother's help Bert soon cut away enough of the meshes of the net so that Flossie could get loose. She was not hurt—not even scratched—but she was frightened and crying.

"There you are!" cried Mrs. Bobbsey, hugging her little girl in her arms. "Not a bit hurt, my little fat fairy! But how in the world did you get in the net, and what is it doing up on top of this hill in the midst of a blueberry patch?"

"I—I just stumbled into it," said Flossie, "same as Freddie got stuck in the mud, only I didn't paddle in the water."

"No, there isn't any water around here," returned Nan. "I can't see what a net is doing here. I thought they only used them to catch fish."

"Maybe they put it up here to dry, as the fishermen at the seashore dry their nets," said Mrs. Bobbsey.

"No," announced Tom, who had been looking at the net, "this isn't for fishes."

"What is it for then?" asked Bert.

"It's for snaring birds. I've seen 'em before. Men spread the nets out on the grass, and over bushes near where the birds come to feed, and when they try to fly they get caught and tangled in the meshes. I guess this net hasn't been here very long, for there aren't any birds caught in it."

"But who put it here?" asked Mrs. Bobbsey. "I think it's a shame to catch the poor birds that way. Who did it?"

Tom looked carefully around before he answered. Then he said:

"I think it was the gypsies."

"The gypsies!" cried Bert.

"Yes. They're a shiftless lot. They don't work and they take what doesn't belong to 'em. They're too lazy to hunt with a gun, so they snare birds in a net. Why, they'll even eat sparrows—make a pie of 'em, my mother says. And when they get robins and blackbirds they're so much bigger they can broil 'em over their fires. This is a bird-net, that's what it is."

"I believe you're right," said Mrs. Bobbsey, when she had looked more closely at it. "It isn't the kind they use in fishing. But do you really think the gypsies put it here, Tom?"

"Yes'm, I really do. They put 'em here other years, though I've never seen one before. You see, the gypsies sometimes camp here and sometimes on the mainland. All they have to do is to spread their net, and go away. When they come back next day there's generally a lot of birds caught in it and they take 'em out and eat 'em."

"Well, they caught a queer kind of bird this time," said Bert, with a smile at his little sister. "And it didn't do their net any good," he added, as he looked at the cut meshes.

"I'm sorry to have destroyed the property of anyone else," said Mrs. Bobbsey, "but we had to get Flossie loose. And I don't believe those gypsies have any right to spread a net for birds."

"My mother says they haven't," replied Tom.

"Let's take the net away," suggested Bert.

"No, we haven't any right to do that," said his mother, "but we can tell the man who has to enforce the laws against hunting birds. I'll speak to your father about it. Are you all right now, Flossie?"

"Yes, Mummy. But it scared me when I was in the net."

"I should think so!" exclaimed Nan, patting her sister. "Did you just stumble into it?"

"Yes. I was walking along, and I saw a bush with a lovely lot of blueberries on it. I ran to it and then my foot tripped on a stone and I fell into the net. First I didn't know what it was, and when I tried to get up I was all tangled. Then I shouted."

"And I helped her call," said Freddie.

"Indeed, you did, dear. You were a good little boy to stay by Flossie. But you're both all right now, and next time you come berrying stay closer to Mother."

"You've got lots of berries," said Flossie, looking at Bert's basket.

"Yes. Tom showed us this good place. And now I guess we'd better go," said Bert. "Maybe those gypsies might come to look in their net."

He glanced around as he spoke, but though it was lonely on this part of Blueberry Island there were no signs of the men with rings in their ears who had set the bird net.

Dinah made enough blueberry pie to satisfy even the four twins, and when Mr. Bobbsey heard about the net he told an officer, who took it away. Whether or not the gypsies found out what had happened to their snare, as the net is sometimes called, the Bobbseys did not hear, nor did they see any of the wandering tribe, at least for a while.

Jolly camping days followed, though now and then it rained, which did not make it so nice. But, take it all in all, the Bobbseys had a fine time on Blueberry Island. Mr. Bobbsey got Flossie and Freddie some new "go-around" toys, and the small twins had lots of fun with them. The old ones they did not find.

Snoop was not found either, though many blueberry pickers, as well as the Bobbseys themselves, looked for the missing black cat. Nor was Snap located, though an advertisement was put in the papers and a reward offered for him. But Whisker did not go away, nor did anyone try to take him, and he gave the twins many a fine ride.

"And I'm glad the gypsies didn't get Whisker," observed Flossie. "I like him. Maybe not so much as I like Snap and Snoop, but I like him awfully well."

"Yes, he's a nice goat. Nicer'n Mike's goat that we 'most brought, but didn't. I'm glad now that we didn't get Mike's goat, aren't you, Flossie?"

"Yes, I am."

The Bobbseys had been camping on the island about a month, when one day Mrs. Bobbsey went over to Lakeport to do some shopping, taking Nan and Bert with her, and leaving Flossie and Freddie with their father. Of course Dinah and Sam stayed on the island also.

But you can easily imagine what happened. After Mr. Bobbsey had played a number of games with the small twins he sat down in a shady place to rest and read a book, thinking Flossie and

Freddie would be all right playing near the big tent.

The two little ones were making a sand city. They made a square wall of sand, and inside this they built sand houses, railways, a tunnel, and many other things, until Freddie suddenly said:

"Oh, if we only had some of the shells that are down by the lake we could make a lot more things."

"So we could!" cried Flossie. "Let's get some!"

So, never thinking to ask their father, who was still reading, away rushed the two twins, after shells.

The place where the mussel shells were usually to be found was not far from the tents, but like most children in going to one place Flossie and Freddie took the longest way. They were in no hurry, the sun was shining brightly, and it was such fun to wander along over the island. So, before they knew it, they were a long distance from "home", as they called Twin Camp.

"Maybe we oughtn't to've come," said Flossie, as she stopped to pick some blueberries.

"We're not so far," said Freddie. "I know my way back. Oh, Flossie! look at that butterfly!" he suddenly called, making a grab for the fluttering creature. The butterfly flew on a little way and Freddie raced after it, followed by Flossie.

"Now I'm going to get it!" the little boy cried. With his hat he made a swoop for the butterfly, and then suddenly he and Flossie, who was close behind him, tumbled down through a hole in the ground, which seemed quickly to open at their very feet, between two clumps of bushes.

"Oh!" cried Freddie, as he felt himself falling down.

"Oh dear!" echoed Flossie.

Then they found themselves in great darkness.

CHAPTER XX

THE QUEER NOISE

FREDDIE BOBBSEY sat down with a thump. Flossie Bobbsey sat down with a bump. This was after they had fallen into the queer hole. And yet it had not been so much of a fall as it was a slide.

Both of them being fat and plump—much fatter and plumper since they had come to Twin Camp than before—the thump and the bump did not hurt them very much.

They had slid down into the hole on a sort of hill of sand, and if you have ever slid down a sandy hillside you know the stopping part doesn't hurt very much. And, after all, the part of a fall that hurts, as the Irishman said, it not really the falling, it's the stopping so suddenly that causes the pain.

"Freddie! Freddie!" called Flossie, a few seconds after she and her little brother had fallen into the hole. "Freddie, are you there?"

"Yes, I'm here, Flossie," was Freddie's answer, "only I dunno 'xactly where it is. I can't see."

"Nor me neither. Are you hurt, Freddie?"

"No, are you?"

The children were forgetting all about the right way to use words, which their mother had so often

161

told them, but as they were excited, and a little frightened, perhaps we must excuse them this time.

"I—I just sort of—of bumped myself, Flossie," said Freddie. "Are you all right? And where are you?"

"I'm right here," replied the little girl, "but I can't see you. I—I—— It's awful dark, Freddie!"

"I can see a little light now," Freddie went on. "Let's get up and see if we can crawl back. My legs are all right."

"So's mine, Freddie. I guess I can——" And then Flossie suddenly stopped and gave a scream.

"What's the matter?" asked Freddie, and the little boy's voice was not quite steady.

"I—I touched something!" gasped his sister. "It was something soft and fuzzy."

"Oh, was that you?" asked Freddie, and his voice did not sound so frightened now. "Well, that was my head you touched. I—I thought maybe it was something—something after me. I didn't know you were so close to me, Flossie."

"I didn't either. But I'm glad I touched you. Where's your hand? I'm sort of stuck in this sand and I can't get up."

By this time the eyes of both the children had become more used to the darkness of the place into which they had fallen, and they could dimly see one another. Freddie scrambled to his feet, shaking from his shirt and trousers the sand that had partly filled them when he had slid down the incline, and gave his hand to Flossie. She had about as much sand inside her clothes as he had, and she shook this out. Both children then turned and looked up at the slide down which they had so suddenly fallen.

Up at the top—and very far up it seemed to them—they could see, at the end of the sandy slide where they had started to slip, a hole through which they had fallen. It was between two big stones, and had a large bush on either side. It had been covered with grass and bushes so that the small twins had not seen it until they stepped right into it. Then the grass and bushes had given way, letting the children down.

"We—we've got to get back up there—somehow," said Freddie with a doleful sigh, as he looked at the place down which he and his sister had tumbled.

"Yes, I would like to get up out of here," said Flossie, "but how can we, Freddie?"

"Climb up, same as we fell down. Come on."

Taking his sister by the hand, Freddie started to climb up the hill of sand. But he and Flossie soon found that though it was easy enough to slide down, it was not so easy to climb back. The sand slipped from under their feet, and even though they tried to go up on their hands and knees it was not to be done.

"Oh dear!" cried Flossie after a while, "I wish we were Jack and Jill."

"Why?" asked Freddie.

"'Cause they went up a hill, an' we can't."

"Maybe we can if we try again," said Freddie. "Anyhow, I don't want to be Jack, and fall down and break my crown."

"You haven't any crown," said Flossie. "Only kings an'—an' fairies have crowns."

"Well, it says in the book that Jack has a crown; an' if I was Jack I'd have one too. Only I'm not and I'm glad!"

"Well, I wish I was Jill, so I could have some of that pail of water," sighed Flossie. "I'm firsty," and she laughed as she used the word she used to say when she was a baby.

"So'm I," said Freddie. "Let's try to get up to the top, an' then we can get a drink, maybe. Only I'd rather be Ali Baba than Jack, then I could say, 'Open Sesame', and the door to the cave would open by itself, and we could walk out and carry diamonds and gold with us."

"I'd rather have bread and butter than gold. I'm hungry. And I'd most rather have a drink," sighed the little girl. "Come on, Freddie, let's try to get up that hill. But it's awful hard work."

"Yes, it's hard," agreed Freddie, "but we've done lots harder things than that." You see, Freddie was trying to keep up his little sister's courage.

Once more the two little twins tried to climb the hill of shifting sand, but they could get up only a little way before slipping back. They did not get hurt—the sand was too soft and slippery for that, but they were tired and hot, and, oh! so thirsty.

"I'm not going to climb any more!" finally said Flossie. "I'm tired! I'm going to stay here until Mummy or Daddy or Nan or Bert comes for us."

"Maybe they won't come," Freddie said.

"Yes, they will," declared Flossie, shaking her

head. "They always come when we're lost and we're lost now."

"Yes, I guess so," agreed Freddie. "I wonder where we are anyhow, Flossie?"

"Why, in a big hole," she said. "Oh, Freddie!" she suddenly cried, "maybe we can get out the other way if we can't climb up."

"Which other way?" asked her brother.

"Out there," and in the light that came down the hole through which the twins had fallen Freddie could see his sister pointing to what seemed another dim light, far away at the end of the big hole. For Flossie and Freddie had fallen into a big hole— there was no doubt of that. Though it was pretty dark all about them, there was enough light for them to see that they were in a cavern.

"Maybe it's a cave, like the one we went into from the lake when we found the boat," said Flossie, after thinking it over a bit, "and if we can't get out one end we can the other."

"Maybe!" cried Freddie eagerly. "Anyway, we can't get up that hill of sand," and he pointed to the one down which they had slid. "Come on, we'll walk towards the other light."

Far away, through what seemed a long lane of blackness, there was a dim light, like some big star, and towards this, hoping it would lead to a hole through which they could get out, the children walked.

As they neared it the light grew brighter, and they were beginning to feel that their troubles were over when suddenly they both came to a stop.

For, at the same time, they had heard a queer noise. It came from the darkness just ahead of them and was such a strange sound that Flossie put both her arms around Freddie, not so much to take care of him as that she wanted him to take care of her.

"Did—did you hear that?" she whispered.

Freddie nodded his head, and then, remembering that Flossie could not very well see his motions in the darkness he said:

"Yes, I heard it. I wonder——"

"Listen!" whispered Flossie. "There it goes again!"

CHAPTER XXI

"HERE COMES SNAP!"

THE sound came once more through the darkness to the little Bobbsey twins, and as they listened to it Flossie and Freddie looked at one another in surprise. They could just dimly make out the faces of each other in the dimness.

"Mamma! Mamma!" cried a voice, for it was a voice that had caused the queer sound; yet it did not sound like the voice of man, woman, or child. "Mamma! Mamma!" it cried.

"Hear it?" asked Flossie again.

"Yes," answered Freddie. "It's a little boy or girl—like us—an' it's in this cave. I guess lots of children get lost here like us. Now I'm not afraid."

"Mamma! Mamma!" came the voice again.

"It—it's kind of funny," whispered Flossie to Freddie. "Don't you think it's kind of funny, Freddie?"

"Yes, but I know what makes it."

"What?"

"It's being in this cave. You know how we used to shout at the hill, when we went to the country —'member that?"

"Yes," answered Flossie.

"An' how our voices used to come back an' sort of hit us in the face?" went on her brother.

"Yes."

"Well, that was an echo," said Freddie, "an' that's what makes it sound so queer here. It's an echo."

"Oh," said Flossie. She had not thought of that.

Once more the voice sounded out of the darkness.

"Mamma! Mamma!"

"There! Hear it? It's an echo!" cried Freddie.

Flossie listened a moment. Then she said:

"If it was an echo, Freddie, why didn't your voice echo too?"

"Oh—er—well—'cause I didn't want it to," Freddie made answer. "I can do it now. Hello! Hello! Hello!" he called as loudly as he could.

And then, to the surprise of the children, back came a voice in answer, and in more than an answer, for it asked a question. No longer did the voice call: "Mamma! Mamma!"

Instead it cried:

"Hello, there! What's the matter! Who are you and what do you want? Where are you?"

Flossie and Freddie were so startled that, for a moment, they could only hold on to each other.

Then Freddie found his voice enough to speak. He said:

"Did you hear that echo, Flossie?"

"That wasn't an echo," declared his little sister quickly. "Echoes only say the same things you say and this—this was different."

"Yes, it was," Freddie agreed. "But maybe it's a different kind of echo."

"Try it again," suggested Flossie, when they had remained quietly in the darkness for a time. And during that time they had not heard the strange voice calling. It seemed to have been hushed after the "echo", if that was what it was, made answer. "Call again," Flossie begged her brother. Once more he called:

"Hello! Hello! Hello!"

"Well, what do you want?" back came a voice in question. This time there was no doubt about its not being an echo. It had not repeated a single word that Freddie had cried.

"Oh, how funny!" cried Flossie. "What makes it do that?"

Before Freddie could answer, even if he had known what to say, the two children saw a light coming towards them. It was the light of a lantern, bobbing about in the darkness, and because it was a light, which chased away some of the gloom, they were glad, even though they had been a bit frightened by the queer voice and the echo which did not repeat words as the other echo had done.

"Oh, maybe it's Daddy and Bert come to look for us!" cried Flossie eagerly.

Freddie thought the same thing, for he called out:

"Here we are, Daddy!"

But, to the surprise and disappointment of the children, a surly voice answered them:

"I'm not your father! Who are you, anyhow, and what are you doing in this cave?"

Flossie and Freddie, clinging to each other, shrank back in fear. Then, as the light came nearer, they saw that the lantern was carried by a tall man. He had gold rings in his ears, on his feet were big boots, and around his neck was a bright yellow handkerchief.

"Oh!" gasped Flossie. "Oh, he—he's a gypsy!"

Freddie saw it, too. The man seemed surprised to see the children. He gave a sort of grunt, held the lantern up to their faces, and exclaimed:

"Why, there's two of 'em!"

"Yes, we—we're twins!" stammered Flossie.

"Twins are always two," Freddie added, thinking, perhaps, that the gypsy man did not know that.

"Twins, eh?" remarked the man in a questioning voice.

"The Bobbsey Twins," said Freddie. "We came from our camp, and we——"

"How'd you get in this cave? That's what I want to know!" cried the man, and he spoke harshly. "Tell me, how did you get here?" he asked, and he held the lantern in front of the faces of the two little children.

"We—we fell in here!" said Freddie, pushing Flossie behind him. He felt that he must look after his little sister and protect her.

"Fell in?" cried the man.

"Yes, through a hole. We slid down a sandy hill, and we couldn't climb back again. We saw a little light over this way and we walked to it and then we heard someone cry: 'Mamma!' Are there any more little children here?" Freddie asked.

"Hum! Yes, some," half-grunted the gypsy. "But not your kind. I don't see how you came here," he went on, speaking to himself, it seemed, for he did not glance at Flossie or Freddie and there was no one else near by. The man looked all about the cave.

"Which way did you come?" he asked.

"Back there," and Freddie, who was doing most of the talking, pointed towards the place where he and Flossie had tried so hard to climb up.

"Come and show me," the man ordered them, and when they walked back with him, the lantern making queer shadows on the side walls of the cave, Flossie and Freddie pointed to the place down which they had slid.

"Hum!" murmured the gypsy. "I never knew there was a way into the cave from there. I must see about that. It wasn't open before. Well, now you're here I've got to make up my mind what I'll do with you," he went on, as he motioned for Flossie and her brother to walk back in front of him. He held the lantern so they could see where to step, but the earthen floor of the cave was smooth, and the children did not stumble.

"Will you take us back to Twin Camp, where we live?" asked Freddie. "We're the Bobbseys, you know, and we didn't mean to run away again, though I guess we're lost. My mother and my daddy will be looking for us, and if you'll take us to the camp——"

"Well, maybe I will after a bit, but not now," said the gypsy, shaking his head so that his earrings jiggled. "You'll have to stay here with us awhile. If you went out now, and told your folks you had found us here we'd all be sent to jail, most likely. I'll see what the others say."

Flossie and Freddie wondered what others he meant, but he did not tell them. He kept walking close behind them, and there was nothing for them to do but to keep on.

Suddenly they turned a sort of corner of the cave, and then the children saw something that surprised them. Seated around a table, on which some candles, stuck in bottles, were burning, were a number of men. They were all gypsies, like the man who had met the children farther back in the cave, and as he walked forward, behind Flossie and Freddie, the other gypsies looked up.

"Who was calling?" asked one of the dark men at the table.

"These two," said the first man, pointing to the little Bobbsey twins. "They answered my call and I found them. They fell down a hole at the far end of the cave, near the sand. I never knew it was there."

"It is an old entrance," put in a gypsy who was eating some bread and tomato, cutting first a slice of one and then of the other with a big knife. "That entrance was overgrown with grass long ago," he added.

"Well, these two stumbled on it," grumbled the man who had found Flossie and Freddie. "We'd better stop it up. And now what's to be done with 'em?"

"We'll have to keep 'em here for a while," said two or three at once, and hearing this, Flossie and Freddie were sad.

"Yes," went on the first gypsy, "we'll have to keep 'em here until we're ready to go, and that won't be for two or three days yet. The only trouble is that some of their folks may find where we have hidden 'em and——"

"Hi!" suddenly cried an old gypsy, and then he said something very quickly, but in words the children could not understand. It was gypsy talk. After that all the men spoke in this same way. Florrie and Freddie felt sure they were being talked about, for the men looked at them many times in the light of the lantern and candles.

Suddenly, when there came a lull in the talk, and the twins were wondering what was coming next, they heard a dog barking. Now, ordinarily, this would not have surprised them, for they knew the gypsies kept many dogs, and some might be in the cave. But there was something different about this bark.

In wonder Flossie and Freddie looked at each other. Then Freddie cried out:

"That sounds like Snap!"

All at once there came a regular chorus of barks, and with them a man's voice could be heard shouting. Then came a dog's growl and yells from a man's voice, then more barks.

"Look out!" shouted someone in the cave. "The dog's loose!"

Flossie and Freddie saw a big dog spring into view from somewhere out of the darkness of the cave, and as the eyes of the twins lighted on him, Freddie cried:

"Here comes Snap! Here comes Snap! Oh, Flossie! our dog that was lost is found! Here's Snap!"

CHAPTER XX

HAPPY DAYS

NO doubt about it. There was Snap, alive and happy. He barked and tried to kiss both Flossie and Freddie at the same time with his red tongue. It was Snap, but he was thinner than when at home in Lakeport, and his nice coat of hair was muddy in some places, and not at all neat.

"Oh, but it's Snap! It's our Snap!" cried Freddie in delight.

"And he found us!" added Flossie. "Now the gypsies can't make us stay here." And standing beside the big dog, she looked boldly at the men who were now standing about the table.

A man came running out of the darkness of what seemed to be a small cave inside the larger one, and cried:

"He broke away! I couldn't keep him any longer. He seemed to hear someone calling him."

"Keep still!" sharply ordered the gypsy who had had the lantern.

"Oh!" exclaimed the other man, as he saw Flossie and Freddie. "Is it their dog?"

There was no need to answer him. Anyone could see that Snap belonged to the Bobbsey twins. He was so happy with them.

"Did you—did you have our dog all the while?" asked Freddie, as he played with Snap's long ears.

The gypsy who had had the lantern said something in his strange language and no one answered. Probably he had told them not to speak.

"Oh, I'm so glad to see you!" cried Flossie. "We looked everywhere for you, Snap. Didn't we, Freddie?"

"Yes, we did. And now we've got him we can go home. Snap knows the way home. He can take us there."

"Oh, no, he can't," said Flossie.

"Why?" asked her brother.

"'Cause he's never been in our tent-camp. He doesn't know where it is. But maybe you know, Freddie."

"Yes, I know the way—if—if we can get out of this cave," and he looked at the gypsies. They were talking among themselves. One of them walked towards Snap and held out his hand towards a broken rope around the dog's neck. But the animal growled in such a fierce way that the gypsy drew back in fear.

Then there was more talk among the men about the children and the dog. The men seemed to be worried. Snap barked and ran a little way ahead, as though to lead the way out of the cave. Again a man tried to catch him, but the dog's savage growl made him draw back.

"I guess Snap wants us to come with him," said Flossie. "Let's go, Freddie."

"All right—come on." And Freddie, taking

Flossie's hand, started out of the cave. They were afraid, the children were, that the gypsies might stop them, but the man who had had the lantern said:

"Come on. I'll show you two the way out and you can go to your camp. No use keeping you, now that your dog is loose. He'd make trouble for us. Hurry up, you fellows, get things out of the way!" he called to the other gypsies, and they began taking things off the table as though they were going to leave.

But Flossie and Freddie did not care about that. All they knew was that they had found Snap, and that they were going home with him to Twin Camp. And Snap was as glad as were they.

"There you are!" said the gypsy in rather a growling voice, as he led the children to where a big patch of sunlight shone into the cave. "I guess you can find your way home from here."

Flossie and Freddie ran on, Snap going ahead, and, to the surprise of the twins they found themselves at the mouth of the cave—the same place where they had taken shelter from the rain the day they were in the drifting boat.

"Why, look here!" cried Freddie. "Isn't this funny, Flossie? We've come out of the same cave we were in before. How did we get in?"

"I don't know," answered the little girl, "'cept maybe it's a fairy cave an' changes."

But it was not that kind at all. The children had only fallen into a hole at one end of the cave, and when the gypsy man led them through they came out at the other end, where they had first gone in. Snap barked and ran down to the edge of the lake to get a drink of water.

"He's glad to come out," said Flossie.

"Awful glad," agreed Freddie. "So'm I."

"Me, too," added the little girl. "I wonder how he got in there?"

"I guess the gypsies took him," said Freddie. "They liked him 'cause he is such a good dog. I'm so glad we've got him back. Now if we could get Snoop back we'd be all right, wouldn't we, Snap?" and he put his arms around the dog's shaggy neck, while Flossie patted his back.

Happy because they had found their dog, and not worrying at all about having been so nearly kept prisoners by the gypsies in the cave, the two little Bobbsey twins hurried away from the cavern. They were anxious to get back to camp to tell the others how they had found Snap. And the dog seemed just as anxious to get away from the cave as were the little boy and girl.

Every once in a while Freddie would turn and look back, and when his sister asked him why he did this he told her he was looking to see if he could see the black cat.

"She ought to be easier to find than Snap," he said, "'cause she was with us here on Blueberry Island, and Snap must have been taken by the gypsies in Lakeport." Afterwards they found that this was so.

As the children, with their dog, walked along through the woods, keeping close to the lake shore, as they knew that path led to their camp, Flossie and Freddie heard a shout among the trees.

"There's Nan!" Freddie said.

"Yes, and Bert," added his sister. "I guess they're looking for us."

They were sure of this a little later, for they heard the cry:

"Flossie! Freddie! Where are you?"

"Here we are!" they answered, and then sounded a noise of someone coming towards them. The next moment Nan and Bert came into view. Both stopped in surprise at the sight of the dog.

"Where'd you get him?" asked Nan.

"Is he really Snap?" cried Bert.

"Yes! He really is," answered Freddie. "We found him!"

"In a cave," added Flossie.

"In a cave?"

"And there were gypsies there," went on the little girl.

"An' they wanted to keep us," said Freddie.

"But they didn't," added Flossie.

"No. But Snap was there."

"And he growled at the gypsy man."

"And he came away with us."

"Snap was awful glad to see us, Nan."

"And here we are now," said Freddie, putting an end to this duet.

"Oh dear!" exclaimed Nan. "This is dreadful! Gypsies on this island, and they almost kidnapped you! You must tell Daddy right away. We've been looking everywhere for you. We thought you were lost again. And you're all dirty and sandy!" she cried.

"That's where we fell down a hole into the cave," said Freddie, and he told Nan and Bert what had happened. Mr. Bobbsey was much surprised when the twins came home with the long-missing Snap. So was Mrs. Bobbsey, as well as Sam and Dinah.

"Gypsies here, are there?" exclaimed Mr. Bobbsey. "Well, I'll have to see about that. We don't want them hiding in a cave and stealing our things. I guess I'll get some police officers and pay the tribe a visit."

But when Mr. Bobbsey got to the cave with the officers the gypsies were not there. They must have known that when the children went out they would tell what had happened and that the police would come. So there was nothing for the police to do. The gypsies had run away. They went to the mainland in boats, some of the blueberry pickers said who had seen them.

"And now that the island is free from the gypsies we'll have lots more fun," said Mrs. Bobbsey. "The thought of them made me nervous."

"Listen!" suddenly exclaimed Nan. She, as well as all the other members of the Bobbsey family, had followed the police to the cave, even Flossie and Freddie going along, riding to the place in the goat-cart drawn by Whisker. "Listen to what?" asked Bert.

"I thought I heard a noise," said the little girl. "Yes, there it goes again, a sort of squeaky noise."

"It's a—it's a cat!" cried Flossie. "Oh, if it should be——"

Before she could finish one of the policemen flashed his flashlight around the sides of the cave, and then, from a dark corner, some animal came slowly out.

"It is a cat!" cried Flossie.

"And it's our Snoop!" added Freddie. "Oh, we've got him back again!"

"Oh, goody!" cried Nan.

"Well, well," said Mr. Bobbsey, "everything is turning out right for you children now."

"And Snoop really was in this cave!" exclaimed Bert.

And so it proved. Whether he had wandered off and had become lost in some little hole of the cave, where he could not get out, or whether the gypsies had stolen him, as they had Snap, the Bobbseys never heard. But they knew they had their black cat again, and they were happy, especially the little twins.

"I want to hug him!" cried Flossie, as the cat rubbed up against her legs.

"So do I!" cried Freddie. "And I want to hug the head part. You can hug the tail end!"

"That end doesn't purr!" exclaimed Flossie. "I want the end that purrs."

"You must take turns," said Mrs. Bobbsey, laughing. "You ought to be glad you have Snoop back instead of quarrelling about him. Well, we have found nearly everything we wanted now, except that bacon someone took the first night."

"I guess the gypsies got that," said Mr. Bobbsey. "It must have been one of them who was sneaking around in the night, and who awakened the children. They probably wanted to have something to eat in their cave. But they've gone now."

"Yes, and they seem to have left something behind them," observed one of the policemen. "I see something white over on one of the boxes they used for a table. Maybe it's only some old papers, though."

Bert hurried over and picked up the white thing.

"It's a doll!" he cried. "Flossie, did you leave your doll here?"

"No," answered the little twin.

"A doll!" cried Nan. "Oh, maybe it's Helen's talking doll! Let me see, Bert!"

But Bert had already pressed a spring and the doll began to call in a queer voice:

"Mamma! Mamma!"

Flossie and Freddie looked at one another.

"That's the noise we heard when we fell into the cave," they said.

"Then the gypsies did take Helen's doll after all, and brought it with them to this island," said Mr. Bobbsey "My, but they are great rascals! They took our dog, our cat, our bacon, the mechanical beetles, and Helen's doll."

"But we've got everything back except the bacon and the beetles," said Bert. "The doll seems to be all right, too, except she hasn't a dress."

"Oh, Helen found that the day she was here on the island," said Flossie. "She found it in an old stump, you know, and I guess maybe the gypsies hid it there, or dropped it."

"I guess so," agreed her mother. "Well, now, isn't this just wonderful! We've found Helen's doll, and your dog and cat. It's a good thing we came to Blueberry Island."

"But I'm sorry the gypsies came here," said Nan. "They made a lot of trouble."

"They've gone now, though," remarked Bert. "It's queer that they brought our dog and Helen's doll here with them."

"Maybe the little gypsy girl, whose daddy took away Helen's doll, brought it here to play with," said Nan.

"Well, everything's come out all right," said Mr. Bobbsey, "and now for some happy days on Blueberry Island, with nothing to worry about." And, indeed, the Bobbsey twins did have very happy times.

Snoop and Snap were back with them again, and with Whisker, the goat, played with the children. Helen was told about her lost doll having been found, and she came to the island to get it.

"Oh, but I just love it on Blueberry Island!" said Flossie, as they all came back to camp from a little picnic in the woods one day.

"So do I," said Freddie. "Now let's hitch up Whisker and have a ride." And they did.

And so I must bring this story about the adventures of the Bobbsey twins to an end. But they had many other good times.

Snap and Snoop had a large part in the good

times, and the dog and cat were none the worse for having been kept in the gypsy cave. Nor was Helen's doll, which the little girl was very glad to get back. It talked as well as ever.

And now I will say good-bye for you to the Bobbsey Twins.